"Ann Major pulls you into the story and doesn't let go…"
—*Rendezvous*

* * * *

"Cheyenne?" He Whispered Softly, Solemnly. "Are You Still Here, My Darling?"

Darling?

He had called her his darling.

She jumped at the gentleness of his husky voice, intending to run.

But he held her there in the soft, hot darkness.

Not with his hands or by any use of force. Not even with more huskily spoken words. His stark gaze was enough to make her know how much he needed her.

If he wanted her that much, she wanted to stay.

She wanted to go on lying with him.

And for a long time they did continue to lie together in the darkness, their legs and arms tangled, neither of them daring to speak again or bat so much as an eyelash for fear of frightening the other away.

Dear Reader,

The celebration of Silhouette Desire's 15th anniversary continues this month! First, there's a wonderful treat in store for you as Ann Major continues her fantastic CHILDREN OF DESTINY series with November's MAN OF THE MONTH, *Nobody's Child*. Not only is this the latest volume in this popular miniseries, but Ann will have a Silhouette Single Title, also part of CHILDREN OF DESTINY, in February 1998, called *Secret Child*. Don't miss either one of these unforgettable love stories.

BJ James's popular BLACK WATCH series also continues with *Journey's End*, the latest installment in the stories of the men—and the women—of the secret agency.

This wonderful lineup is completed with delicious love stories by Lass Small, Susan Crosby, Eileen Wilks and Shawna Delacorte. And *next* month, look for six more Silhouette Desire books, including a MAN OF THE MONTH by Dixie Browning!

Desire…it's the name you can trust for dramatic, sensuous, engrossing stories written by your bestselling favorites and terrific newcomers. We guarantee handsome heroes, likable heroines…and happily-ever-after endings. So read, and enjoy!

Melissa Senate

Senior Editor

Please address questions and book requests to:
Silhouette Reader Service
U.S.: 3010 Walden Ave., P.O. Box 1325, Buffalo, NY 14269
Canadian: P.O. Box 609, Fort Erie, Ont. L2A 5X3

ANN
MAJOR
NOBODY'S CHILD

SILHOUETTE Desire®
Published by Silhouette Books
America's Publisher of Contemporary Romance

To Ted, my husband; To Tad , my son, for the book material;
To my mother, for her love and sweetness;
To Lauren, my niece, who told me about Brazil;
To Anita and Tara, for their professional guidance;
To Kimberly, my daughter, for making the dean's list;
To Dr. Michael Heckman, my doctor, for mending my knee and
reassuring Ted I would ski again;
To David Cleaves and Diana Gafford, for being there;
To Ann Engel, the megatalented Realtor who not only sold my house
but became my new best friend and therapist.

 SILHOUETTE BOOKS

ISBN 0-373-76105-8

NOBODY'S CHILD

Books by Ann Major

Silhouette Desire

Dream Come True #16
Meant To Be #35
Love Me Again #99
The Wrong Man #151
Golden Man #198
Beyond Love #229
In Every Stranger's Face #301
What This Passion Means #331
*Passion's Child #445
*Destiny's Child #451
*Night Child #457
*Wilderness Child #535
*Scandal's Child #564
*The Goodbye Child #648
A Knight in Tarnished Armor #690
Married to the Enemy #716
†Wild Honey #805
†Wild Midnight #819
†Wild Innocence #835
The Accidental Bridegroom #889
A Cowboy Christmas #967
The Accidental Bodyguard #1003
*Nobody's Child #1105

*Children of Destiny series
†Something Wild

Silhouette Special Edition

Brand of Diamonds #83
Dazzle #229
The Fairy Tale Girl #390

Silhouette Intimate Moments

Seize the Moment #54

Silhouette Romance

Wild Lady #90
A Touch of Fire #150

Silhouette Books

Silhouette Christmas Stories 1990
"Santa's Special Miracle"

Silhouette
Summer Sizzlers 1992
"The Barefooted Enchantress"

Birds, Bees and Babies 1994
"The Baby Machine"

Silhouette
Summer Sizzlers 1995
"Fancy's Man"

ANN MAJOR

loves writing romance novels as much as she loves reading them. She is the proud mother of three children who are now in high school and college. She lists hiking in the Colorado mountains with her husband, playing tennis, sailing, enjoying her cats and playing the piano among her favorite activities.

A LETTER FROM THE AUTHOR

Dear Reader,

As a little girl, born and raised in south Texas, my favorite game was riding broom horses and playing cowboys and Indians. As a teenager I spent a lot of time visiting my small-town cousins who had horses. We fed them and rode them and loved them. My closet is still filled with jeans, cowboy boots and Stetsons. No myth is greater or grander in Texas than that of the cowboy.

Perhaps it is only natural that I wrote my CHILDREN OF DESTINY series, which deals with the Jacksons and the MacKays—modern ranchers, who were the descendants of great pioneer ranching families. Once I began writing about these mythic people, I couldn't stop.

Nobody's Child continues the series with the passionate love story of Cheyenne Rose, or Witch Girl, an enchanting woman of mysterious powers, and the dangerous entrepreneur, Cutter Lord, whom she loves even though he is determined not to love her.

Then next comes *Secret Child,* out in February 1998 in time for Valentine's Day. Once again I write about a modern-day cowboy and the woman he loves.

When Jack West's wife vanishes, no one knows that she hired a plastic surgeon to change her face. Five years later, through a bizarre twist of fate, a young kindergarten teacher, Bronte Devlin, loses everything—even her face. When the same plastic surgeon who helped Jack's wife gives her the face of the most beautiful woman in the world, Bronte finds herself in terrible danger. Forced to masquerade as her dangerous double, Bronte is abducted by Jack and soon finds herself fighting for her life as well as for the heart of this rugged rancher whose real wife turned his heart to stone.

I hope you enjoy *Nobody's Child.*

Sincerely,

Ann Major

Prologue

The night was black and wild. The wind was so fierce that every flower and leaf in Texas had blown off all the trees.

Cutter Lord, who lived life on a dangerous edge, was driving way too fast. He was used to delegating unpleasant errands. Not that he hadn't tried to delegate the troublesome Miss Rose, but his younger brother's unsuitable fiancée had bested his top man.

"You'll have to deal with Miss Rose yourself, or else—" Paul O'Connor, his vice president, had thundered, rubbing his bruised wrists on the steps outside the Dallas city jail after Cutter had bailed him out. Paul was black and smart and tough, and not easy to scare.

"Or else?"

"I quit. The lady snuck up behind me with a vase of the biggest purple pansies you ever saw, hit me with it and locked me in her gardening shed. I nearly froze before she called the cops."

Cutter was used to chauffeured limousines...to the luxury of his private jet...to other people shouldering all the hassles when he traveled. Which was often. And to far more glamorous places than south Texas.

Not tonight.

As if hurled by the brute force of the worst winter storm to hit Texas in ten years, the hail-dimpled, black Lincoln and its grim driver shot from the mainland onto the narrow causeway that led across the Laguna Madre to the barrier islands.

The radio said the windchill was now minus ninety degrees in Crookston, Minnesota, and that two hundred cars were stranded on Nebraska roads. Tornadoes had ripped off roofs in Arkansas, Oklahoma and Texas. In the panhandle the temperature had dropped forty degrees in two hours. Three people had died in windstorms near El Paso.

The devastating norther that had closed the Dallas airports and grounded Cutter's jet was roaring into the humid warmth of the state's southern coast with bands of gale-force winds and icy rain.

Cutter Lord, who preferred to spend his nights in a warm bed with a beautiful woman, was bone-weary from having driven too many miles on ice-slick highways.

One woman was responsible for Cutter's foolhardiness. One woman had so infuriated him that he had lost all his judgment. Thus, he and the storm raced toward the island together, like two angry giants, determined to trample whatever got in their way.

With his ebony hair, black eyes and strong dark face, Cutter was blessed with the kind of virile good looks most women found exciting. He was six-two, lean, and powerfully built. He had brains, drive and an iron will. His fierce dedication to his family's business was legendary. His friends attributed his astounding success to his *genius* and high energy levels. His enemies said he was ruthless. The bottom line was that he usually made money. Lots of it.

Suddenly—ahead—the causeway vanished into a dark, inky froth. Brake lights flashed as cars began to back up.

Hell. The tide was rising and surging inland.

Instead of turning back, Cutter inched forward into the

purple waves. He had to hurry, before the authorities closed the causeway—the only road to the barrier islands and, thereby, to Cheyenne Rose.

He'd come this far; he wouldn't let anything stop him from dealing with Miss Rose.

Every time he remembered *her* midnight call, his blood ran colder than a shark's on the trail of blood. She hadn't liked his calling her a gold digger.

Her husky voice had had the taunting, singsong quality of a nursery rhyme.

Fight, fight, as hard as you can. If I want to marry your baby brother, Mr. Lord, you can't stop me. I'm the gold digger girl.

She had giggled as she tossed his taunt back at him, "the gold digger girl."

Then she had laughed again.

At him.

"You know what your problem is, Mr. Lord. You're spoiled!"

Cutter's hand had clenched on the receiver, his nostrils flaring even as some part of him had dissolved in her velvet voice.

Then—right before she hung up—she had purred, "Oh, by the way, Mr. Lord, I had your mean, tough Paul O'Connor arrested for peeping into my bathroom window—he's handcuffed to a metal chair beside a prostitute down at the city jail. Just thought you'd like to know. Also, I've left town so I can decide without any more interference from you whether or not I want to marry Martin and become your *sister*."

His sister! The hell she'd be his sister!

Cutter had slammed down the phone and demanded to know one thing once Paul verified she had, indeed, left town.

Where the hell was she?

Within an hour his men informed him that Martin had flown her to the beach house on Lord Island, and that she planned to stay there all by herself for a week.

All by herself.

On Cutter's remote private island off the Texas coast.

Perfect.

Or it would have been except for the storm.

Cutter wasn't afraid of her. Nor of a mere storm. And her call had only made him all the more determined to stop her.

Only now, he had to do the dirty work himself.

Spoiled?

He wasn't spoiled!

He just had to win.

The black waves in the Gulf had risen to Goliathan heights. Not that they were that big in the protected marina.

"Boss, you shouldn't go till morning," Miguel screamed above the howling wind as Cutter untied a dockline. "Maybe not then."

"Right. Like I drove all night through sleet and hail so I could sit the storm out in a Port A. bar or a cheap motel."

The boat, which Martin had named *Jolly Girl* one sunny summer day, was the only way to reach Lord Island tonight.

Fight, fight as hard as you can—

Damn right, he'd fight her as hard as he could. Cutter would fight because he knew he'd go mad if he had to listen to her singsong voice flit through his brain till morning.

When he jumped from the dock into the bucking sloop, he slipped on the wet fiberglass and almost fell. He opened the hatch and began casting off.

"*Loco*," Miguel yelled frantically. "You crazy, boss. You don't know enough about boats. Your brother Martin—"

Cutter glared at him.

Cutter was a remarkable entrepreneur.

He was a less than remarkable yachtsman.

Not that he could have ever admitted there was anything he couldn't do better than his playboy brother.

Cutter stubbornly primed the bulb and then pushed in the automatic choke before starting the engine.

Only when Cutter cast off the last line, and the little boat hurtled free of the dock into the purple waves, did Cutter begin to doubt the wisdom of having let anger and arrogance rule him.

But by then it was too late.

Almost immediately, the lights of the shore and Miguel's alarmed cries were lost in the troughs of black waves and driving rain.

The cold wind tore at his foul weather gear, and rain rushed inside it. Cutter's teeth began to chatter as he headed toward his island.

An hour later, the little engine coughed and died. It had made almost no headway against the wind and the waves. He heard the crashing surf and knew he was too close to shore. The electricity on the island had gone out, and without lights to guide him, without the motor, he'd never make the channel to the island's man-made harbor.

He had to restart the motor. But as he leaned over the stern, a large wave slammed into the boat, foaming into the cockpit. When *Jolly Girl* lurched violently, Cutter lost his footing and slid overboard. As the cold rushing water swallowed him, he fought to reach the surface.

One gurgling breath. Then he gulped water as another wave crashed over him and dragged him under.

He clawed his way through the darkness to the surface again.

This time he didn't quite make it and gulped salt water instead.

As he sank, he heard the taunt of *her* husky purr.

Mr. Lord, you can't stop me. I'm the gold digger girl.

She was laughing at him as he kicked against the undertow that sucked him down, down, ever deeper into a cold, wet hell.

A feeble sun broke through the gray, making the calmer waters glimmer like polished silver.

Waves curled around a man's bare foot.

Freezing. Hungry. Cold.

Freezing. Hungry. Cold.

Again and again like the feeble tattoo of a drum, the words fluttered through Cutter's tired brain.

Cutter was barely conscious. His skin was pale, his lips blue. His shoes and most of his clothes had been torn off. Grit and sand filled his wet black hair, nostrils and ears. Every time he tried to swallow, his throat burned.

He had lost all sensation in his legs and arms and fingers and toes.

Where the hell was he?

Who cared? He was so cold, he just wanted to sleep.

Forever.

Then he heard a husky cry that was somehow familiar.

"Oh, my God—" A woman's terrified voice.

With great effort he opened his eyes and saw the upturned hull of *Jolly Girl.*

But he wasn't looking at the wreck. A breeze whipped a gauzy, white skirt high up a pair of shapely legs.

A woman.

Cheyenne Rose.

The troublesome witch blurred in a red haze of pain as if she were no more than the figment of a nightmare.

He forced his heavy burning eyes open again.

She wasn't what he had expected.

She was slim and lovely—as lovely as her voice. She had a sweet face. An enormous, white gardenia bloomed in her hair.

He shivered violently, not wanting to like her.

What the hell was the matter with him? Was he delirious? Dying?

It didn't mean a damn that she was pretty. Or soft and vulnerable looking.

She was the enemy.

But it did…mean a damn. He felt something deep and hot and eternal grip his heart.

As if she were a child clutching a treasure, she held a

bag of shells in one hand as she stretched on tiptoes to examine the wrecked hull.

Her long red hair blew around her face and neck. She was dressed in a white sundress. A silver light came from behind her and lit her hair like spun flame. There was something fragile and otherworldly and enchantingly angelic about her. He noticed that behind her the sand dunes were ablaze with Fiddleleaf morning glories and yellow sunflowers as if it were summer.

What kind of woman came to an island and stayed there through a violent storm and then got up the next morning to hunt seashells?

She had fine, delicate features with high cheekbones and the greenest eyes he'd ever seen. Her breasts and hips were deliciously rounded; her waist small. Her skin was pale gold, and as she stared at the boat and him with wonder and fear, he realized that she was not only smolderingly sensual but irresistibly innocent.

He groaned as a sudden pain convulsed in his chest.

Startled by his cry, she screamed and jumped back. Her wary green eyes studied him. Then her incandescent smile dazzled him.

He shut his eyes.

She hesitated a brief moment before racing toward him. Conserving the last of his strength, he lay very still.

Until she reached him.

"Hello?" Her husky voice grew more anxious. "Everything's going to be okay."

She was an enemy to whom he should show no mercy. In answer to her greeting, his large brown hand snaked around her slender ankle and yanked hard.

Her shells flew, scattering on the sand. With a muffled cry, she toppled onto him.

He gasped with pain from her weight across his chest. Then he rolled over, so that his body crushed her.

His black, gritty hair dripped sand all over her pretty, pale gold face. All over her small, freckled nose.

His intention was to terrify her.

"I'm sorry I scared you," she said and then she sneezed and dusted sand from her nose. "Sorry..."

He said, "Bless you."

He noticed how warm she was. It was as if she'd brought summer with her.

He felt dizzy. Then he pitched forward. For a second, before he fainted, he felt the warm cushion of her breasts and the silken touch of her fingers gently stroking his hair.

When the blackness receded, he was wrapped in thick blankets. She had made a fire from driftwood and was bending over him and smiling anxiously. "Do you think you could drink some hot coffee?" she urged. "Then maybe in a minute, if you could try to walk, and I think you can...because I examined you...while you were unconscious, we could get you into the house. I've built a fire inside, too, and I'm sure by now it's warm there."

He smiled warily, teeth chattering, as she poured the coffee and lifted his head and brought the plastic mug to his trembling lips.

He sipped obediently.

When he was done, she said softly, sweetly, "Oh, good. Please, don't be afraid. You're hurt. And I want to help you. We have to get you out of your wet clothes. What's left of them, anyway..."

Their eyes met again. She blushed shyly, her skin glowing like an angel's.

He drank more coffee, the whole thermosful, and the warmth of the liquid filled him—or was it just the radiance of her smile that made winter change to summer?

He had never met anybody like her.

She was putting her arms around him and struggling to help him sit up when her sweet face blurred around the edges as once more he dissolved into a dizzying blackness.

His last pleading words to her were, "Don't leave me."

Cutter had never spent so much time lying down, being waited on and pampered. He had never wanted to.

For three days he had dwelt in a room scented heavily

with gardenias and other summer flowers while Miss Rose had nursed him.

And he had relished every minute.

His enemy.

But, oh, how he had loved her coming to his bedroom to tend him with her gentle hands and her kind voice.

More than loved it. In his weakened state he had longed for it. Pined for the wild gardenia scent of her.

And every time she came into his room smelling of summer flowers, smiling and carrying another steaming tray of delicious, spicy hot food, he felt consumed by an inexplicable tenderness toward her. Did she flavor his meals with some magical ingredient that made it easy for her to charm him?

He had thought his beach house with its far-flung wings and modern lines too remote and boring to ever visit.

He never wanted to leave it now.

The phone was out. He found he liked feeling cut off from the world, his business, and from civilization. From the rigid rules that governed him, from the rules that made Miss Rose a highly unsuitable wife for a Lord.

The house seemed a natural thing atop the fragile dunes. It seemed to blend with the high wavy golden grasses that grew near it as well as with the salt marshes and their pungent, dank-smelling ponds behind the dunes. Each day since the storm had been warmer and more summery than the last. Now the island with its soft humid breezes and white beaches seemed to be weaving a lazy spell on both of them. Flowers bloomed everywhere. She gathered them in baskets and brought them inside.

Wrapped in a blanket, Cutter got out of bed and went to his chaise lounge near the fireplace and the window. He saw Miss Rose lying outside in the sun on his vast deck. Protected from the wind by a wall of sheer glass panels, she wore a skimpy white bikini while she pretended to read one of her grisly spy thrillers.

She had the most abominable literary tastes. She went for genre paperbacks with lurid covers that featured half-naked people or lethal weapons, lightweight novels that always had happy endings. "Page turners," she'd called them when he'd criticized. Page turners, hell— He knew that she was only pretending to read. He'd been watching her for an hour—indeed, he couldn't take his eyes off her any time she was near. She hadn't turned a single page.

He eyed the clock on the wall impatiently.

Two-thirty. Soon she would get up as she had every other afternoon.

Odd, how eager he was for her sunbath to end. For her to come back inside.

To him.

This avid craving was ridiculous.

They had absolutely nothing in common.

She read trash.

He preferred business journals, news magazines, newspapers and the occasional, really good literary novel.

"Newspapers and literary novels are depressing," she had said.

"One should stay informed."

"One should have fun, too."

"Was that why you dropped out of college?"

"No. I told you. Mother got sick, and I had to help her. I wanted a degree more than anything."

He hadn't had the heart to tell her that his finance degrees were from the best eastern schools.

She was a struggling caterer. He hadn't told her he was a multimillionaire. Nor had he told her his family had been wealthy and socially prominent for generations.

And, of course, he hadn't told her he was Cutter Lord, her fiancé's *spoiled* half brother.

Nor had she confessed she was a small-town bastard from Westville, Texas. That her mother had been called Alligator Girl and Witch Woman, that she, Cheyenne, had hung out in the salt marshes tending to her mother's gators and strange wild things until she was eighteen. Then there'd been some sort of trouble, and she'd left home forever.

No, his private detectives had told him all that.

She had told him that she loved flowers and all wild things.

He eyed the clock again.

Sometimes when she finished her sunbath, she walked on the beach.

Cutter, who had lain there willing her to come inside for more than an hour, smiled triumphantly when she got up and peered anxiously through the window. He beckoned her inside.

She opened the door, her body flushed from the sun, her smile bright and teasing, her red hair and the dune flowers in it mussed. At the sight of her, a wild rhythm started in his chest.

She met his gaze and looked away. "You have to stop doing that."

"What?"

Breathlessly, she said, "Looking at me that way."

"I thought you liked me to." He got up and moved toward her, trailing his blanket across the bleached pine floor.

"I—I..."

"What's the matter?"

Frightened, she began backing. "There's something I have to tell you."

"So—tell."

"I'm practically engaged to another man."

"Do you love him?"

The beach morning glories quivered in her hair. The tiny scar beneath her left eye, which was the only blemish on her near-perfect face, whitened. "Of—I'm not sure."

"So—how do you feel about me?"

Her frantic eyes burned into him the same way her spicy food did.

"I have to know," Cutter insisted.

"His brother doesn't want us to marry. He doesn't think I'm good enough. I—I came here to be alone— To think about Martin and our future together." Her eyes glistened with unspoken pain as she studied Cutter. "Not for—"

"Not for this." With one hand Cutter grasped her shoulder. With his other, he caught her red hair and flower petals. His mouth slanted across hers.

Her lips parted hesitantly; he felt her soft, indrawn breath. Next she shocked him by the full heat of her response to his kiss as her tongue slid against his. Consumed by hunger, his arms tightened around her slim waist as she surrendered passionately.

"Cheyenne—"

"No!" She stiffened and drew back. "Please—" She threw the door open and ran.

"Damn," he muttered, watching her, not following even though he sensed that if he pressed her now, he could win. He was tempted to go after her, to pull her into the sand and seduce her. Then he could tell Martin and advise him that Lords didn't marry easy women like her.

But three days with her had robbed Cutter of the appetite to destroy her.

She had been so nice to him.

She had saved his life.

Which meant he owed her. Yes. But how much?

Surely not Martin's future and fortune.

There was a new wrinkle. Cutter now wanted her himself.

Torn, Cutter hesitated—and that wasn't like him.

Why the hell didn't he just seduce her?

It was only later that he wondered if he had not sensed the impending danger *she* would be to his coldly ordered life. To his soul.

But—until he met Cheyenne Rose, Cutter had not known he had a soul.

Until Cheyenne he had glided through life. First as the precocious, brilliant son and dutiful brother. Then as the ruthless businessman who believed that life was about money, not love. He had married; divorced. But ultimately, always—until Cheyenne—he'd been alone, an outcast. Envied and never loved. He had sought admiration. Not love. His loneliness hadn't mattered—until her.

Arrogant to the core, Cutter was accustomed to the glitter of exotic capitals and the easy pleasures of beautiful women. Long ago, when he had become strong enough to crush his opposition, he had not imagined that anyone, least of all a girl, could ever crush him.

Cutter had lived in many houses and in many foreign lands. He had made many fortunes and had had many women. But nowhere and to no one had he ever belonged, least of all to himself. He spoke many languages, but not one of them was the language of his own soul. He'd had little understanding of those weaker than himself. He had not cared that his younger brother felt jealousy for him instead of love.

And then Cutter had washed up on his island, and she had turned the tables on him by saving his life. His cynical world and all its rules had changed.

Not completely.

Because when she had asked his name, he had lied and said, "Lyon."

Cheyenne was wearing her bikini and holding her paperback and gauzy cover-up, but she couldn't work up the nerve to go out on the deck for her daily sunbath.

Because Lyon was somewhere outside.

She couldn't see him.

Or let him see her.

Lyon had avoided her ever since he'd kissed her yesterday, and she was grateful to him for that.

And yet, somehow, his absence made her think of him even more.

Whenever Lyon came near the house, she kept to Martin's elegant bedroom with its long windows and dark blue walls and white throw carpets and paintings of the sea.

But she felt miserable and trapped as she stared, with white-knuckled fingers against the shuttered windows, out to the sea and the primroses in the dunes and wondered where Lyon was. She wanted to go out and lie in the sun and listen to the surf and think.

Did she have an hour before he came back?

She wanted to love Martin. Only Martin. Why then did thoughts of Lyon possess her? Why had the dune flowers started to bloom the moment she'd seen Lyon?

This couldn't be happening.

She couldn't let it.

All her life Cheyenne had wanted to legitimize herself, to be somebody, to marry someone who *was* somebody, to have the normal sort of life and family her half sister, Chantal, and so many people were born with and took for granted. To be accepted, valued—

But more than anything, even such a life, Cheyenne now wanted Lyon.

He was a stranger. She knew almost nothing about him.

He was a good listener, but he had revealed very little about himself.

What was he hiding?

He couldn't hide the fact that he wanted her.

She had felt the hot physical bond almost from the first moment when he'd lain freezing and hurt and helpless on the beach.

Martin must never know.

She shivered in disgust. How could she think like that even for a second?

Because she was illegitimate, everybody in Westville had said she was trash. All her life Cheyenne had tried to live down the taint of her birth. She hadn't dated because every time she looked at a boy, people said she was as bad and strange as her odd, fast-living mama, Ivory Rose.

As Martin Lord's wife, everybody would admire her. She could go back to Westville with a grander name than the Wests, her father's "real family." Chantal could no longer act so superior. If she, Cheyenne, had her own husband, maybe it would no longer matter that Chantal had married Jack, the young boy whom Chantal's mother had rescued from the barrio so many years ago. Ever since then, he'd used "West" as his surname.

Before coming to the island Cheyenne had told Martin

she hadn't made up her mind about marrying him. She'd told his odious brother the same thing.

Not that she'd thought there was much to think about. Jack was lost to her forever. Boyish and charming, Martin was the nicest guy she'd met since she'd escaped Westville.

Until Lyon.

A smart girl wouldn't consider marriage to a stranger who'd washed up on a deserted beach. Even if he had made flowers bloom.

Distracted, she continued to stare outside.

Nothing. Just golden grass and white sand. And endless wildflowers. Yesterday Lyon hadn't come back all day.

She decided to risk an hour on the deck.

Carefully she tiptoed outside where she took off her gauzy cover-up and swam several laps in the sparkling pool. The water was too cold, so she got out and dried off and lay down on a long white towel.

After a few minutes the warm sunlight drugged her senses.

She didn't hear him approach.

Suddenly *he* was just there, blocking the sun—a huge male animal, bronzed and magnificent, his legs thrust widely apart as he loomed over her as if he were a dark giant from a fairy tale.

She twisted her head and looked straight into his starkly handsome face.

And suddenly Martin and all her dreams of a new life vanished.

There was only Lyon. Only this moment and this sharp need. Only this fierce recognition of her other half.

She saw her own desire mirrored in his fiery eyes and for the first time in a long, long time, all the lies she had told and lived since she had run from Westville to Dallas melted away. She didn't know who he really was, and she didn't care. His naked, lonely soul reached out to hers and re-created her into some truer self that had longed to exist but had lacked the courage to be until she had formed this incomprehensible bond with him.

Still, when she got up on shaky legs, and he held out her gauzy cover-up, she ran from those outstretched brown hands and from him.

But he had seen the truth in her glowing eyes, or maybe just her desire.

Whatever. He chased her.

Panting, she locked herself inside the patio doors.

But she stood there just inside, expectantly staring at him from behind the shining glass—waiting excitedly.

"Go away," she whispered even as some deep and truer part of herself challenged him to unthought-of needs and violent deeds.

A huge piece of driftwood that she had found on the beach the first day before the storm and lugged to the deck glistened in the sun at his bronzed feet.

Easily he leaned down and picked up the limb. Then staring into her eager, wide gaze for a long moment, he lifted it high above his head.

Transfixed, she watched as the muscles of his arm bulged before he hurled the wood against the glass, smashing it.

The explosion of zillions of slivered shards of flying glass dazzled her.

Or was it just Lyon?

When he kicked a few shards aside and strode across that ruined threshold, his shoes made crackling sounds in the glass. She just stood there, as frozen and still as a statue while her blood sang with a silent, shocking wildness.

There was no wind, but a powerful force whipped the sea oxeye, sunflowers and sea oats. Suddenly more summer flowers burst forth into bloom.

She knew she should have run and fought and struggled.

But when he seized her and wrapped his body around hers, when his lips came down hard on hers, claiming her in that most basic and eternal way, she could deny him nothing.

She had never existed before his hot mouth made her flame into being just as the dune flowers had.

Nor had he.

Both their lives had been lies.

Nothing on earth—not all the precious dreams and ambitions she had lived on since a child, not even her dream to be as grand as her sister—mattered in the face of Lyon who had become the master of their mutual reality.

Lyon—who was he?

She didn't know.

She only knew that even as his hands shredded her bikini and tore the bra from her breasts, even as he ripped off his ragged jeans and shirt, she would belong to him forever.

Even if all he ever wanted from her was sex.

She had hungered for her own respectable identity ever since she'd been five and her sister had first branded her with the word *bastard*.

She had thought money and marriage would give her the security and the respect she craved.

Lyon was everything.

She would be whatever he wanted.

For as long as he wanted. With or without marriage.

He was hers. In that single shining moment, as he held and kissed Cheyenne, they burned with the same flame and everything was very simple.

Only later did it become so complex and terrible.

Cutter made no sound as he lifted her and carried her across the litter of white carpets, up the swirl of stairs, to the bedroom that looked across the dunes to the sea. He took time to open all the doors, so that the surf roared in their ears, so that they could smell the salt and feel the damp wind against their hot, naked bodies. Then he fell across her on the bed and, with one fist grasping her long red hair, he shaped her to him and plunged inside her.

They came together violently, in quick, fluid thrusts, like a primitive couple, their bodies sparking, rising and falling in the wildness of the ancient ritual.

They took no time to know each other.

Both were shocked.

He to discover that this wanton whose golden body responded to him with such primitive eager response was a virgin.

She to discover that pain could open the floodgates to ecstasy and knowledge of another's soul.

They didn't speak.

Not then.

Not later.

There were no words.

They needed no words.

They just loved. Sometimes with their bodies fused quietly. Sometimes they twisted and writhed.

All that afternoon.

Into the brief glow that is a southern twilight on a windswept beach.

And again during their long, single black night together.

Endlessly.

Completely.

But, ah, so devastatingly.

And when it was over, the island was even hotter than it ever got in full summer. Bees buzzed above the dune flowers. Cicadas sang as if under a spell.

The man and the woman lay wrapped together, each sure that, whatever happened, she could never, ever marry Martin Lord.

One

Nothing sells like celebrity murder.

Especially not on a humid, spring night in Houston, Texas, when lilacs and wisteria as well as wild water lilies have suddenly decided to bloom early—and all these magic blossoms are three times their normal sizes.

Thus, the hottest ticket in that southern city of skyscrapers, freeways and sluggish brown bayous on that cool Saturday night was the Martin Lord bankruptcy auction at the Castle Galleries in the city's fashionable Southwest.

Quite naturally everybody, absolutely everybody, attended. The Wests from their great ranch, El Atascadero, near Westville and Theodora West's even more famous ranching cousins, the Jacksons from their far grander ranch, were there *en masse*. Mercedes and Wayne Jackson, Amy and Nick Browning, as well as Megan and Jeb Jackson had all come. Yes, the rich, the greedy, the overdressed, the envious, as well as the merely curious were there to watch and to gloat at the widow's latest humiliation, as one by one, Cheyenne's most beloved and most prized possessions went on the auction block.

The gossips buzzed.

Had she killed Martin?

Or had his older brother?

There had always been gossip about Martin and Cheyenne Lord even before Martin's chain-draped, nude body had washed ashore on an oyster reef in Galveston Bay six months ago. Even in Houston, the youngest, brashest city in Texas where flamboyant behavior on the part of the city's rich is almost a duty, the couple, who had lived both extravagantly and scandalously, had continually raised the bar of vulgar excesses.

Take the Lords's wedding seven years ago at the Jackson Ranch in south Texas when Martin had gotten roaring drunk and ridden one of Jeb Jackson's prize bulls up the aisle to take his vows. Not to be outdone, the groom's older brother had stormed in late during the reception and forced the bride to kiss him. And not a brotherly kiss, but a kiss so electric with white-hot passion that every single guest had been charred by its carnal sizzle. Indeed, Mrs. Gilchrist, a gray-headed society matron, whose seat had been the closest to the embracing couple, had told everyone who would listen that wisps of steam had arisen from her very own cuticles for as long as the couple's lips remained fused.

Fortunately before Mrs. Gilchrist's fingernails could be completely eviscerated, Cheyenne had fainted in Cutter's arms. The rogue would have carried her off, had not the groom and his groomsmen seized Cutter by the throat and hurled him to the ground. They might have killed him, if Jeb and Tad Jackson hadn't pulled them off and rushed the unconscious Cutter Lord to a hospital.

Cutter retaliated by seizing control of his younger brother's fortune and firing Martin from Lord Enterprises. Thus, had it not been for Martin's rich friends, the newlyweds would have begun their lives together almost penniless.

There had been more talk when Cheyenne had delivered a strapping, ten-pound son with a shock of ebony hair less than eight months later.

Even more talk when Cutter had showed up in the hospital nursery and possessively glowered down at the baby that looked so alarmingly like him and then exchanged cruel, damning words with the new mother who had almost died giving birth to the boy he claimed as *his* son.

The baby had started to cry, and Cutter had picked him up. Then as the child quieted, Cheyenne had burst into tears, and when Cutter had tried to take her into his arms, too, Martin had summoned security. Cutter had been dragged away.

There had been even more talk when Cutter had refused to back down from the financial decisions he had made regarding Martin, and the brothers failed to patch up their quarrel.

Things had quieted down a bit when Cutter had moved to the south of France, and Martin and Cheyenne Lord, aided by loans, had settled into their vulgarly stylish marriage and endeared themselves to the city by planting a magical garden and throwing frequent and flashy parties at which the bride always served her wonderfully spicy food.

The talk had resumed, however, when the bride's married sister, the flamboyant Chantal West, had left her husband, Jack West, and seduced Martin on Cheyenne's front lawn. The gossips had had a field day with the rumors Chantal started about Cheyenne. Soon everybody knew that the sweet, sad-faced Mrs. Martin Lord, whose flowers grew bigger than everybody else's and whose exotic herbs had a taste all their own, had never had a daddy to claim her. Chantal reported that Cheyenne's mother had been a tramp who raised gators, cast spells, cooked for cowboys and slept with whichever one she took a fancy to.

It was the notorious Chantal who first made everybody aware how the weather in Houston always got warmer and how trees bloomed out of season after every Lord party. How everybody got a little crazy, too. How couples who hadn't slept together in years would go home and make love to each other all night long.

Martin Lord, who had an obsession for upstaging his rich brother, had liked notoriety of any sort. Thus, he hadn't discouraged his mistress from gossiping about his wife's strange powers and scandalous past. Martin, who'd had a Texas-size ego and a mania for media attention, had gotten himself proclaimed the leading real-estate tycoon in the state. He had had an enormous import-export business as well. His wife had become a celebrity caterer and the author of five wonderful, bilingual, coffee-table cookbooks. Still, there were those who said they could see beneath Cheyenne's beauty and sophistication to the wild bad blood that they now knew raced in her veins. Everybody said that no recipes were richer or spicier or hotter than hers. But what really made her books off-the-chart bestsellers was that rumor Chantal had started about Cheyenne's food having aphrodisiac qualities.

The Lords had lived high. They owned a mansion in Houston's best neighborhood, a showplace ranch in south Texas, and a villa on a high cliff in Acapulco.

They'd lived like kings. In spite of the gossips.

Right to the end.

But Martin Lord had died broke.

No.

Worse than broke.

Martin Lord had left his lovely widow and son, Jeremy, millions of dollars in debt, five million to be exact, to dangerous people on both sides of the border.

But the most dangerous enemy she had, at least as far as Cheyenne Lord was concerned, since her heart and soul were involved, was her brother-in-law whose searing wedding kiss was so well remembered. Especially by Mrs. Gilchrist whose fingernails had never quite recovered.

Tonight Cheyenne had given orders that Cutter was not to be sold a ticket to the auction; nor was he to be admitted should he dare try to make an appearance.

Still—tonight when she'd stepped out of her house and was about to get into her limousine, she hadn't been able to ignore two rather alarming signs. A single bolt of lightning had arched over her head, scrawling a white *C* in a cloudless black sky. At the very same moment her magnolia tree, which had shed its last blossom the day of Martin's death and had been barren ever since, had suddenly burst into bloom.

Cheyenne had read in these simultaneous happenings a sign.

Cutter Lord was definitely on his way.

She had slammed her door with a vengeance, fighting to catch her breath. Why was it still so maddeningly easy to remember their time on the island? Especially that moment shortly before dawn when she had cupped his face between her hands and stared deeply into his eyes, marveling at their warmth after he'd just confessed his love for her?

For her public lynching, Cheyenne had chosen to wear a skintight, black leather pantsuit and a soft black cashmere sweater that fit her like a glove. Her necklace and earrings were fashioned of serious diamonds and emeralds, a wedding gift from her husband. His only gift in seven years of marriage. Not that she had wanted another.

As the widow greeted the Jacksons, her good friends who were effusive in their friendliness, and then Theodora and Chantal West, her father's "real" family, who were as chilly as iced champagne, Cheyenne hoped none of them noticed that her hand with the diamonds shook and that her frequent smiles were quivery as she scanned the crowd for Cutter.

Theodora, who had never before said Ivory Rose's name aloud to anyone other than her deceased husband and then only in anger, thawed a little and murmured how sorry she was that Cheyenne's dear mama was so ill.

Ivory Rose had suffered a stroke the day Martin had been found dead, and was confined to her bed with round-the-clock nurses, which Cheyenne was struggling to pay for.

Cheyenne's eyes shimmered. "But I thought...that you disliked her—"

"I—I used to think so, too. But relationships are not always what they seem. I was jealous." Theodora moved closer and put a hand on her shoulder. "I couldn't help it.

She was a free spirit. She was so much younger and so much more beautiful."

"I really hated to leave her...so sick," Cheyenne murmured, touched. "As soon as this is over, Jeremy and I will definitely go back to be with her."

Theodora's thin, cold hand lingered consolingly. "I never thought I'd say this, but I'll miss her more than I'll miss most people in Westville." For one brief moment Cheyenne felt that maybe, just maybe, her father's family might someday feel affection for her.

Then Chantal spoke. "My, my, Witchgirl." Her soft voice was somehow more predatory than her fierce eyes. "How sweet you always are, *dear* sister."

The two sisters looked at each other, saw themselves in each other's faces and, as always, were unpleasantly jolted.

Cheyenne remembered growing up in Westville. There had been an unspoken competition between the rich and icily controlled Theodora West and her husband's mistress, the fun-loving Ivory Rose who hadn't minded at all that she'd had an awful reputation or that some of the townspeople thought she was a witch. Their competition had spilled over to their daughters because the two women had used them in their silent war with each other. Every school contest in which both girls entered had been a battle, and every time Cheyenne, the wild child, had bested her sister, the ranch princess, which had been often—and there had been those who said that witchcraft had given her the edge—Chantal had found some terrible way to get even.

Tonight Chantal's color was high. As always, she was too intensely involved with Cheyenne, especially now that the spotlight was on her.

Although Chantal was flamboyantly sexy in a tight red sheath, and had never looked lovelier, she exuded a dangerous aura of resentment and insecurity because people had come to see Cheyenne, not her.

More than anything on earth Chantal wanted to be the star. Cheyenne's stomach tightened. Chantal had married

Jack and seduced Martin to get revenge. What might she do next?

Had their mothers not been such polar extremes, Chantal would have hated her simply for existing. Chantal especially resented their too-startling resemblance, perhaps because it proved their kinship. Perhaps, because having a double made her feel less special.

Still, if only their mothers hadn't pitted them against each other, maybe they could have become real sisters.

No.

Cheyenne had given up on that dream. Never again would Cheyenne try to impress Chantal or the Wests. After tonight Cheyenne was through with being in the public eye, with caring about others' opinions. Cheyenne would be finished with men, with love, with marriage and, therefore, hopefully, with this sister who had betrayed her twice.

Cheyenne wanted only her precocious son.

She wanted peace and solitude.

And safety.

For an instant she remembered Cutter's dark, tortured face when he'd held and soothed Jeremy so tenderly right after his birth. The baby had taken to him, cooing and gurgling happily almost instantly. Cutter's expression had softened when Jeremy had wrapped his little hand around Cutter's finger. She had thought then how warm and lovely it had been to have his child. She had wanted the moment to last forever. When Cutter had looked abruptly from the baby to her, she had wanted him in her life so much, she had begun to weep. Even now she still wondered what might have happened if Martin had not been there.

No.

She wanted a magnolia tree without blossoms.

Theodora West left before the auction started. The Jacksons sat in the row behind Cheyenne. Chantal West vanished into the crowd just as the auctioneer began the sale with Martin's valuable Tang horse, which went quickly.

A few lots later, the gavel pounded down so hard Cheyenne could almost feel sparks flying. Soon she forgot all about Chantal.

"Sold to the highest bidder," cried the skinny auctioneer with the vulgar yellow tie.

Again all eyes turned to the dazzling redhead in black cashmere, who paled, the words having stung her like a whip.

Cheyenne felt as if she was dying by inches as two men rolled up a Persian carpet that had been in her bedroom and dragged it off the stage. But she kept her expression a careful blank as the bidding resumed.

She felt numb, so numb that the sounds and visions blurred. Would this nightmare that had become her life never end?

"Do I hear a thousand—"

Only a thousand.

Cheyenne, who was sitting in the center of the first row, flanked by her son and bodyguard, jumped up. She seized the microphone and began to describe how she and Martin had come to possess the particular antique crystal vase on the block. As she spoke, guests suddenly saw or thought they saw dozens upon dozens of tall yellow roses blooming and growing ever taller in the vase that now looked both magical and wonderful.

When she handed the microphone back to the auctioneer the bidding leapfrogged as it always did after such a poignant anecdote and strange occurrence.

Cheyenne's green eyes glassed over again as she sank into her chair once more and folded her perfectly manicured hands together with a pretense of calm.

She was used to pretending. She had grown so very, very good at it during the seven years of her miserable marriage, which had been one of public glitter and private humiliation.

But ever since Martin's murder—no, even six months before that, when the telephone death threats had begun—it had grown harder to pretend.

It was on that day that the magnolia tree had first started

to shed its blossoms. It became totally bare the day Martin had been found.

A single magnolia petal had fluttered downward outside the window as Martin had answered that first call in their dining room with its soaring columns and its Steuben chandeliers and the table that was encircled by eighteen antique gilt chairs. She had watched the magnolia petal until it disappeared. Then she focused on Martin's eyes, which had dilated with fear. Immediately after the brief call Martin had been gray and silent.

"Martin. Please, Martin. Tell me what is going on," she had pleaded as another white petal slid lazily to the ground.

"It's none of your damn business." As his voice echoed with cold finality, white petals began falling like rain.

"But you're my husband."

"Am I?" He came to her then, raised his hand and lifted her chin in a proprietary manner. "In what sense?" he sneered. "I never think of myself as *your* husband. I'm surprised you do."

Somehow she managed not to flinch as his hand stroked her. "Why won't you give me a divorce then?"

His gaze was level and hard. "Because you are my only asset that my brother covets. Besides, of course, *our* son— *the genius.*"

"Don't call him that!"

"Have you forgotten our little bargain—darling?"

Words from the past, Martin's proposal, came back to her.

We both hate him. There's only one way to get even with the bastard—by marrying each other.

Martin had referred to their bargain, and she had replied, "Never...for a moment."

But she hadn't hated Cutter. She had merely felt lost and afraid. For the sake of her son, Jeremy, she, who had wanted to be loved and valued, had settled for so much less.

"Good." His voice had softened when he saw that he had her under control once more. He had even smiled at

her. Something he had rarely done when they were alone.
"Relax, darling. Go outside and pick flowers. Work in your
garden. Baby Jeremy. Or let him read to you. Damn it. Do
what you do." He touched her again, indifferently, his fingertips moving from her chin to her throat in a sinister
caress. "This trouble is temporary. I'll bring Kurt home to
look after you and Jeremy. He's been around. You'll be
safe with him."

Even though Kurt was a top man in Martin's business,
she hadn't liked him. Kurt had a brutish face with a
smashed-in nose and cold eyes. His overlarge head seemed
to melt into his powerful, barrel-like torso without benefit
of a neck. Every time she thought of him, red roses blackened, mosquitoes grew to the size of bumblebees and kit-
tens quit purring.

"I'm afraid of him."

Martin's caressing fingertips combed her hair dismissive-
ly. "He's fine."

"Martin, in the name of God, what's going on?"

"Why should I tell you?" Martin withdrew his hand.

She felt numb and blank with regret as Martin grabbed
his briefcase and newspaper and went past her out of the
house. Not that such feelings were new. Every morning
since she'd first discovered him with Chantal and had realized that he hated her, Cheyenne had awakened with the
same blank feeling of hopelessness and the same dull ache
of despair. Later, when the numbness became punctuated
with fear, she had known that as long as Martin had refused
her a divorce, there was nothing she could do about it.

They had never really been married. She had always
been his prisoner, his hostage in the psychological war he
waged against his brother.

If Martin had hated her for sleeping with Cutter and giving birth to Jeremy, he hated her a hundred times more for
costing him control of his fortune. All Martin's problems
had stemmed from his borrowing money to prove to her
and the world that he was as financially brilliant as Cutter.

When Martin had suddenly died, she had felt that her

longed-for release had come—but at a terrible price. She had been shaken to the core by the savage nature of his murder and by how utterly alone she felt in her dangerous trap. Jeremy had been devastated. The little boy had loved Martin in spite of Martin's mood swings from indulgence to sarcasm and neglect. Immediately after his funeral the phone calls had begun, and she had discovered that Martin's death had put Jeremy in terrible jeopardy.

As she sat among the guests and listened to the auctioneer offer her cherished possessions for sale, she wondered if the person making the threatening calls was here, too—watching her. Watching…Jeremy. Waiting for the right moment?

Dear God.

She forced herself to hold her head high, even though her regal posture just made her feel more exposed.

She kept twisting her diamond rings. She kept patting Jeremy's silky, black head, reassuring herself that as long as her precocious darling was beside her with his nose in an encyclopedia, he was safe.

But she couldn't be with him all the time.

She kept remembering the caller's scratchy voice. His terse warning that afternoon.

"You know what I want. If I don't get it, Jeremy's next."

As always the voice had been emotionless and deadly.

"I don't have five million!" she had screamed.

"I like passion in a beautiful woman," he had murmured. "I look forward to meeting you in person."

"Never."

"Soon." He had hung up, but his final threat had replayed itself in her mind dozens of times.

Dear God.

What had Martin gotten them into?

What was she going to do about it?

Run away? Start over? As she had when she'd left Westville all those years ago?

Dear God, how she wanted to.

But where?

How?

With the police interrogating her?

With Martin's creditors hounding her?

With her own career in jeopardy because of the negative publicity? Not that she could concentrate enough to experiment with recipes, plan parties or write. Not that she could ever, if she worked the rest of her life, make enough to pay what Martin owed.

When she had cautioned Jeremy to beware of strangers, he hadn't understood the danger. Laughing, he had said, "If one tries to get me, I'll bash him with an encyclopedia or climb up the magnolia tree."

If anybody other than Martin or herself was responsible for her terrible predicament, it was Cutter Lord. She would never have had to marry Martin, if it hadn't been for Cutter who had used her as he had used so many women. She had been so hurt and afraid, she had made a terrible mistake. Martin would never have had to live so high, if he hadn't been trying to prove himself to Cutter.

How she wished she could loathe Cutter. From the beginning, his behavior had been despicable. Incapable of love or honor, he had seduced her and abandoned her. Then when she'd found out she was pregnant and married Martin, Cutter had been apoplectic.

For Jeremy's sake, Cutter could have helped Martin when he'd asked for help shortly before his death. Instead Cutter had stuck to the brutal terms of their father's will and said he would keep control of Martin's fortune until Martin was thirty-five. She had gone to Cutter and pleaded with him, too, pointing out that Cutter had taken everything from Martin.

Cutter had seized the gigantic rose she'd worn in her hair, and brought it to his nose. He inhaled deeply. "No, Cheyenne. Martin took everything from me. And you helped him do it." He had paused, studying her face and then the rose. "But, hey, sure, I'll be glad to help." Another pause. "For a price. If you ask me sweetly." Then

Cutter had put his hands on her in a hateful, intimate way and propositioned her.

Dear God, she had wanted him to love her.

All he had ever wanted was to use her.

The auctioneer's cry never ceased. An hour later Jeremy's book lay closed on the floor. He began to droop sleepily against her arm. When he tugged at her sleeve and pleaded in a whining tone that he wanted to go home to bed, she kissed his brow and reluctantly ordered Kurt, whom she had never had the courage to fire, to drive him.

As always Kurt's cold stare before he took Jeremy by the hand unnerved her. She felt as if it were winter, and every blade of grass, every leaf, and even the root systems, had withered and died in her garden.

But she stayed.

For she had been told that her presence at the auction added substantially to the money her belongings would bring.

Hour after dreadful hour she sat ramrod straight in her hard-backed, gilt chair.

When the intermission came, she was too exhausted to make small talk. Jeb and Megan Jackson escorted her to a shadowy corner of the bar. Then mercifully they left her to talk to Amy and Nick Browning, and she found herself alone.

But not for long.

For suddenly Cutter Lord was there.

Two

Maybe it was the booze.

Whatever. Cutter Lord was unaccustomed to the sense of uncertainty that filled him the minute he saw *her* heading toward the bar where he'd been hiding for more than an hour.

Pale, creamy skin.

Black cashmere over softly swelling breasts and taut nipples.

So many years.

And he still felt the same.

Cheyenne's eyes were warm and welcoming to everyone she saw and spoke to on her way toward him.

But that would change, the minute she saw him.

He swallowed what was left of his drink.

He should pounce on her now.

Instead he clung to the safety of the shadows and wondered what the hell to do next. The only other times in his life he had been at such a complete loss had been that moment just before dawn on the island when he'd known he'd fallen in love with her and then that single other time when he'd held his tiny son in his arms in the hospital and stared at her with such fury and longing that he'd made her cry.

Suddenly the happier memories of that long-ago night on the island swamped Cutter. He had awakened just before dawn to find her naked body curled trustingly in his arms. He had gotten up, feeling excited and surprised at the strange tenderness he felt toward her, at the regret to leave her in bed alone, even so briefly.

In confusion he had stared out at the ghostly glimmer of gray fog that shrouded the island. Then she had padded silently across the room and gently taken his hand.

At the touch of her slim fingers closing around his, his spirits had rocketed, and all his loneliness, as well as the certainty that she was the wrong woman for any Lord, especially him, had vanished.

Even as he had fought the power she had over him, he had wondered why he had ever thought she was unsuitable when she was the only woman who would do for him. He had kissed her forehead, her drowsy, thickly lashed eyes, her tousled red hair. He had wondered why he had ever thought money could matter between a man and a woman who had felt and shared what they had felt.

Then they had begun to talk as if they had known each other their entire lives. She had told him of growing up in a small Texas town, of having a father who would not claim her, of having a half sister who hated her and who had been determined to best her, of having a beautiful, wild mother the whole town sneered at, of learning to like books with happy endings because her own life had not been so happy.

And he had told her something of his life, too—of the great loneliness he had known ever since he'd been a boy. In fact, he had shared so much in those swift, fleeting moments, telling her everything about himself that had really mattered—except his real name.

They had scampered down to the kitchen as if they were children and made a hasty breakfast of cold biscuits and milk and orange juice. And that simple shared meal had been wonderfully exciting because she was there, feeding him with her fingers.

Then they had raced back to bed and made love again.

He had known then, that for better or for worse, he had fallen head over heels in love with her.

Then she had used her love to destroy him.

Now it was his turn.

Normally Cheyenne didn't drink, but tonight she felt like it. She was ordering Scotch on the rocks, when Cutter's silken baritone came from behind her.

"Make mine a double."

Her smile vanished. Her green eyes turned to shards of ice.

"The wages of sin must be paid, Cheyenne. The devil always claims his due."

But did he have to show up at the worst possible moment?

For an instant the world stopped spinning.

She whirled.

There—behind her in the shadowy dark stood the devil himself. He was twirling a twin red rose to the one she'd worn in her hair the last time she'd seen him.

Cutter's obsidian black eyes locked with hers as he handed her the rose. In his gaze she saw the same bleak, unforgiving emotion she'd seen on her wedding day. The same bleak, loveless emotion she'd seen that last afternoon when she'd begged him to save Martin and he'd seized her rose and then leaned forward and unbuttoned her jacket.

"Sure. I'll be glad to help," he'd murmured in that same softly rough tone. "For a price. If you ask me sweetly."

He'd twisted her second button loose, and she'd felt his warm fingers against the swell of her breasts. She'd gasped and grown instantly hot from his touch.

Some part of her had wanted him to strip her there and then. It had taken her a second or two to gather her wits. She had grabbed the gaping edges of her jacket, and tried to run. But he'd seized her, and pinned her between a wall and his long lean body, until she'd gone limp and breathless from his nearness. Only when her lips had parted, inviting his mouth to touch hers, had he laughed softly and let her go.

He seemed even more hatefully dangerous now.

Never in a million years could she ever forgive him.

Not that he cared.

Tall and broad-shouldered, he loomed over her.

A drop of blood bubbled from the tip of her finger where a thorn from his flower had pricked her. Angrily she threw the rose at him, but it just bounced off the lapels of his tuxedo.

Reality was back with a vengeance.

"My darling sister-in-law," he purred. "You're hurt." Before she could resist, he had her injured finger in his grip and had lifted it to his lips and kissed it.

Dear God. The tenderness of his mouth stung her fingertip with pleasurable shock.

She blushed.

"You look even lovelier than you did the last time I saw you." He brought the scarlet blossom to his nose and inhaled.

As he had done before.

"Your face is as red as my rose," he murmured with insolent mischief.

Her heart pumped wildly. She was too furious to speak, so she tried to run.

He held on to her hand. "Easy does it." He smiled lazily. "Remember me. I'm all bark and no bite."

If only he were so harmless.

He was tough as nails. In his whole life he had never loved another human being. He used women for sex. He stomped on any man who opposed him. Especially his own brother.

Cutter's face looked harder and leaner than it had been seven years ago, but he was still sinfully handsome. The

sheer, raw animal magnetism he projected in his black evening clothes left her breathless.

"How did you get in?" Pulling her hand free, she fell
backward against the solid oak of the bar. "I gave very
specific orders—"

"I'm sure you did." He shot her that hot, beguiling pirate's grin that had seduced so many women. "You forget.
I prefer to give women orders, not serve them."

"You..." The vile word didn't come easily.
"You...bastard."

"No, honey—" His charming, piratical grin broadened,
reminding her of her own questionable parentage.

While he ordered drinks, Cheyenne's mind flashed backward.

*"Mexican!" the kids had jeered on her first day of
school, making her conscious of how dirty and ragged she
was. Only they'd said something that sounded more like,
"Mez-kin."*

"She's the witch's bastard," Chantal had taunted.

*Through her tears, Cheyenne had stared at the ground,
which was dry and cracked and covered with a fine pink
dust that dusted the scuffed toes of her brown boots. Thus,
she hadn't seen the tall, black-haired boy, pushing his way
through the other children. Thus, her first awareness of
Jack West, her first playmate and friend as well as first
love, had been his rough, yet strangely pleasant voice.*

"Leave her alone!"

"Stay out of this!" Chantal had cried.

*Jack, whose blood was half Mexican, too, whose parent-
age was even more questionable than Cheyenne's, Jack,
who had had to fight for his own precarious social position
in Westville even harder than Cheyenne, had yanked Chantal's red braids hard. "Cállate, celosa. You're just jealous
'cause she's your sister."*

*"She's not my sister! I hate her! I hate you, too. She's
just like you—a barrio brat!"*

*"No. She looks like your father. Just like you, too, gringa.
That's why you hate her."*

"No! No!" Chantal covered her ears with her hands.

The bartender set down their drinks.

The adult Cheyenne froze as Cutter placed a crystal glass of straight whiskey into her shaking hand.

"Cheers, Cheyenne. You've come a long way...since Westville. Since my island. Since your marriage to *my* brother. This may be your best party yet. I find I'm enjoying it way more than your wedding even though I haven't yet had the pleasure of kissing you."

Cutter's gaze lingered on her lips, and she remembered her wedding day. Her heart had felt about to break when he'd angrily kissed her. She'd fainted with joy and hope only to be cast down into despair when she regained consciousness to find him gone and Martin there, demanding to know if she wanted to chase Cutter or stay with him.

What choice had she ever had?

Cutter had wanted her, but for sex, not for marriage.

"You look good in emeralds. Too good," Cutter said. "Widowhood becomes you. Too bad you're not yet desperate enough to sell me what I want." He picked up his rose and twirled it. He brought it to his lips and then took a deep breath, drawing in its scent before setting it down again.

His heavy-lidded eyes slid lazily from the rose to her lush mouth, down her body, admiring her generous curves and slim waist.

Even the odd, tentative flicker of desire that went through her annoyed her. He was a sexist, arrogant bully! How could he have this sensual effect on her?

Please, God. Not sensual. Not tonight!

She balled her hands into fists. He read her flushed face like a book and laughed, his overabundant conceit and good humor restored. Without a word he threw his dark head back and easily tossed down his own drink.

"Cheers," she muttered shakily as she tried to toss her drink down with equal aplomb. But the whiskey strangled her and made her cough.

With an excessive pretense of polite concern, he whipped

out a monogrammed handkerchief, and then pounded her hard on the back, and yet not too hard.

When his warm hand stayed in the center of her back, her bare skin beneath the soft black cashmere began to itch and burn.

She sputtered, swallowed more of the awful whiskey and caught another drowning, scalding breath.

"You shouldn't have come," she rasped.

"I was worried about you. I came to offer my services."

The innuendo in his low voice further infuriated her. Rudely she snatched his handkerchief and dabbed at her sweater.

"No. What's more likely is that you couldn't bear to miss my social execution. How did you get a ticket anyway?"

"Chantal."

"I should have known. She's always made my life miserable the same way you did Martin's."

Cutter frowned. "Is that what you think?"

"What do you really want?"

"Many things." His eyes were hot.

He picked up the rose. This time he trailed the soft petals across her lips. "Your body is at the top of my wish list. So is your soul."

She shoved his flower aside. "I shouldn't have asked."

He broke the stem, and placed the flower behind her ear. "I'm glad you did. I want the boy." His eyes drifted over her in that maddeningly, heated way that made her seethe. "You. Everything. And I'm willing to pay exorbitantly."

Pay? The word cut more deeply than he knew.

She didn't doubt that he genuinely wanted Jeremy. But what did he really want from her?

They studied each other. She with hurt and fear and an odd resentment that her father had never once come to her mother and tried to claim her as Cutter was trying to claim Jeremy. He with an intensity that unnerved her.

"I'm asking you to marry me, Cheyenne," he said quietly.

Flushing, her hand clenched the brass bar rail. "You hate me."

His dark brows lifted. "We both wish."

"I couldn't bear another loveless marriage."

"Then we'll pretend."

"No!"

His black head tilted to one side as he studied the sudden sadness in her eyes and the rebellious tilt of her chin. "You are the mother of my only son."

"You refused to help me or Martin when—"

"I underestimated Martin's problems. I was very, very angry at you. I'm sorry. I behaved badly that day—"

"Sorry? Martin's dead and you're sorry? For all I know, you killed him!"

The color leached from Cutter's cheeks, leaving his hard face as waxen and pale as her magnolia blossoms in the moonlight. His good humor vanished, and he seized her. "I was mad as hell at you when you came to me that afternoon, looking so sweet and sexy, pleading for Martin. That's why I did and said those things. But I have an alibi the night of the murder. Do you?"

"That woman who said she was with you all night would say or do anything to please you."

"Most of the women I've dated would," he muttered smugly. "You are the exception. But I didn't kill Martin." His heated gaze wandered from her face down her body.

She closed her eyes to shut him out.

Abruptly he let her go. "Honey, you don't have a whole lot of options."

"And you do. All those redheads, each younger and more beautiful than the one before. Even Chantal."

"None of those other women were the mother of my son."

First she hadn't been good enough, so he'd seduced her to ruin her chances with Martin. Now he only wanted Jeremy.

"Were you jealous...of those other women?" he goaded softly.

"No!"

"Too bad. I damn sure wanted you to be."

"Well, I wasn't!" Why did she spit the words at him then? Why did she see visions of lightning branding the sky above her with a *C* and her magnolia tree bursting into full bloom?

"So—I didn't live like a monk. What did you expect? You got married."

"It was your fault I had to marry Martin—" She stopped herself.

He watched her in silence, a new tension in his pose. "Go on."

"Nothing…"

When he kept looking at her in that strange, intense way, she flushed. "You think you're so smart. You figure it out."

"Well, I got lonely," he finally said. "I am a man. But, if it matters to you—if you accept my offer—I won't complicate our situation with other women. You have my word. And no matter what Chantal told you, there has never been anything between Chantal and me. I took her to dinner. Twice. I asked her about Martin. And about you." He paused. "I wanted to know what your life was like before you got married—"

"How could you go to Chantal?"

"How could you marry *my* brother and keep *my* son from me seven damn years?"

To survive. To protect Jeremy from the kind of unbearable childhood she'd had.

"As if that's my fault! No doubt you want revenge against me for that! You want to hurt and humiliate me—"

His face hardened. "I want Jeremy. You're part of the package."

Even though she knew it was impossible to make him understand, she had to try to explain one last time. "Cutter, the last thing I want is another marriage of convenience. I want to be free. I want to pay off Martin's creditors and run."

"You don't have any money. I do. I thought your ambition was to be the wife of a wealthy man."

"I want my own life now. And to be my own person."

"Unfortunately, it's a little more complicated than that. Martin's killer is an exceedingly dangerous man. If he doesn't get his money, he will track you down and kill you." When she stared at him in mute horror, he continued. "If you don't care about your own life, do you really want to risk Jeremy's—"

"God—" Something inside her broke. He had no way of knowing that ever since Martin's murder she'd had constant nightmares about Jeremy. "You don't play fair, do you?"

There was a hard-driving fear in his face. "It depends on the game, honey. I can't gamble when the stakes are my child's life...and yours."

No matter what he said, he didn't care about her. He never would. He just wanted Jeremy. She had been used in that game of tug-of-war too long not to know that truth.

Tears welled beneath her lashes. She felt hounded from all sides. Her husband had been murdered. Her mother was dying. And her son's life was in danger. Still, she couldn't bear for Cutter to know how near she was to the edge.

"I just want this nightmare to be over," she whispered.

"It's just beginning, Cheyenne. For both of us."

In her mind's eye, she saw a great thornbush take root in her garden and begin to grow at a frantic pace like Jack's bean stalk in the fairy tale until it had smothered every other plant as well as her mansion.

"Don't say that!"

"Wishing for the moon won't make it fall from the sky. You're a strange lady, with strange powers. But you're in one helluva fix. I want to help you."

She felt his fingers brush her cheek. Gently he tried to turn her face to his.

She hesitated, liking his hand there too much, knowing that it would be all too easy to need things from him that he could never give. She jerked away. "Accepting your terms would be like selling my soul to the devil."

"Ditto, honey." His voice hardened.

"If you hate me, why... Why do you now want—"

"I identified Martin in the morgue. Remember? I saw what they did to him. It's no secret I want to sleep with you. Because of Jeremy, I'm willing to marry you. I'll protect both of you."

She couldn't forget that Cutter had abandoned her when she'd most needed him. That ever since, all he'd ever done was insult or publicly humiliate her.

She caught a tight breath. Her voice was cold. "But who... will protect me from you?"

The auctioneer climbed up to the podium and banged his gavel. At the same moment Jeb and Megan called to Cheyenne.

"I have to go," Cheyenne whispered.

"Not yet! I'm not through with you!"

She spun on her heels like a dervish, the scarlet rose flying out of her hair. "Oh, yes, you are!"

Even though she was wild-eyed with panic, she paused to stamp his flower into pulp with her sparkly black shoe.

Their gazes locked. His was black with raging emotions. Hers was filled with fear.

She hated her own helplessness and his easy power over her.

"You stay away from me, Cutter Lord! And Jeremy, too! You are the last man on earth I would ever marry. The very last! Don't come to me with any more of your sordid bargains! Jeremy doesn't want you any more than I do! You'd just ruin his life—the same way you ruined mine!"

"When you calm down, call me at the Warwick Hotel."

"I'll never, *never* call you!"

"Honey, like I said before—you don't have a whole lot of options."

Tears filled her eyes as she turned from him and ran.

* * *

Cutter watched Cheyenne's slim retreating figure with a mixture of explosive fury, wounded pride and utter exasperation.

He wanted her too much. Women always sensed when they had the edge. She'd definitely use it to try to bring him to his knees. She'd married his brother to get even, hadn't she?

"Damn!"

She was always running out on him. Rejecting him. He never chased after women who didn't want him.

Cheyenne Rose had always been the exception to every rule.

She was way too quirky for him. He went for sophisticated, well-read women. Women who'd gone to the best schools. Women who read *real* books, not cheap, paperback thrillers with insipid, pleasant endings. Women of class and breeding who had impeccable reputations and lived without a hint of scandal in their lives, women who did not draw attention to themselves and distract him from the main thrust of his life. *Controllable women.*

Cheyenne was a bold creature of incomparable dazzle. She could dress, too. Not that she ever looked quite at ease with the rich set. Yet maybe that was why she stood out. Maybe that was why he was drawn to her. He had always sensed that beneath the dazzle, she was hurting inside.

Still, she was trouble with a capital *T.*

He had always known it.

She had treated him abominably.

Still, her vulnerability touched a wellspring deep within him. Her seemingly sweet and ingenuous nature enchanted him. And in bed, no other woman came close.

After his divorce he had never thought he'd consider remarriage, but he couldn't get over Cheyenne.

Chantal had once told Cutter that Cheyenne's mother had been so weird people had thought she was a witch, that Cheyenne had lived with this mother in a ramshackle house on the edge of a marsh where tropical plants had bloomed in her garden while the surrounding landscape had been arid.

Sometimes he wondered if there was something to Chantal's outlandish stories. Maybe Cheyenne had stuck a pin in a doll and cast a spell on him. Maybe she simply represented his one failure and, thereby, had remained a challenge. Maybe—

Cutter leaned down and retrieved his ruined rose. It felt heavy and lumpish in his callused palm. Tossing the broken bits of stem and petal into an ashtray with pretended indifference, Cutter ordered another Scotch.

But he was not indifferent.

As always Cheyenne had smelled of flowers. Tonight her heady scent of magnolia blossoms had made his pulse tick faster. Even if she wasn't a witch, every cell in his body ached for her. He hated himself for his weakness, but he was through fighting it.

Not that he wanted to marry her any more than she wanted to marry him. Indeed—she was the last woman he wanted to tie himself to. All he wanted was to bed her till he got as bored or disgusted with her as Martin apparently had. But there was Jeremy, who adored her, to consider. She could help Jeremy accept him. Nor could Cutter stand the thought of another man ever owning her again. And there was the danger. If he didn't step in, she would die.

Cutter had several reasons for attending the auction. One was to buy Cheyenne's possessions so he could return them to her. Thus, he should have felt angry every time she stood up and spoke into the microphone during that long night to drive up the prices. Instead, his heart quickened with a powerful unwanted emotion each time he heard her husky voice.

She was a user and a taker. She had wanted glitz and glamour—more than she had wanted him. She had thought he was some penniless drifter who'd washed up on the beach. She'd slept with him and gotten pregnant and then married his brother because she had thought Martin the better catch. Greed was a vice Cutter understood better than most. Little had she guessed that Cutter had controlled Martin's fortune and could cut them off without a dime.

Still, for a while, she had had everything her way. She had put her past behind her. She'd had her grand marriage. Martin had used the Lord name and his "expectations" to borrow money and invest. She'd had her name in all the magazines and newspapers. She'd made friends with prominent Texans such as the Jacksons. Even the Wests—her father's family who had always shunned her—had attended her parties.

Cutter had tried to forget her. But when she'd given birth to his son and passed him off as Martin's, she had crossed a line. Cutter had stared through the glass at the hospital nursery at Jeremy with a fierce and terrible longing. He had believed then that he could never forgive or forget her. He had wanted to hurt her as she had hurt him. Then he had held Jeremy, and she had wept. Ever since that moment, the longing for his son, and for her, too, had grown stronger. But the years had passed. She had stayed with Martin, and Jeremy had grown up without knowing his real father.

Cutter had lived in Europe, made enough money for a hundred men, slept with the most beautiful European beauties. Other men had envied him, but always he'd felt the same loneliness he'd felt growing up in his parents' strife-torn marriage and in all those soulless boarding schools. Deep down he had wanted a real family and a home.

Not that he'd believed he could ever have that sort of life. Thus, he'd thrown himself into his work, but there had not been a night during those seven years that he hadn't thought of Martin and Jeremy and Cheyenne without envying Martin his perfect family.

Cheyenne thought she drove a hard bargain.

She thought she was going to make him pay dearly to get what he wanted.

Maybe it was time he showed her that he could play hardball, too.

Even if Ivory Rose was on her deathbed, everyone knew the kind of woman Ivory had been in her prime.

Her daughter was no different. Cheyenne had proven she was for sale.

It was time he showed the world she was that kind of woman. All that was left was to determine her current market price.

There was a lull in the bidding as a set of English Wedgwood china was placed on the block.

Once again Cheyenne arose and took the microphone, but before she could begin what was sure to be still another poignant tale about how precious those damn dishes had been to Martin, several guests pushed their chairs back with a yawn.

The show was beginning to bore people.

Not for long. Cutter felt a furious urge to get even with Cheyenne by humiliating her publicly.

From the back of the room, Cutter's deep, liquor-slurred voice rang out. "For the person of Mrs. Martin Lord, and not a single one of those damned sissy dishes with the pink roses on them—I offer one million dollars. In cash."

Everyone swiveled in their chairs. An expectant hush fell over the crowd. He met their openmouthed stares with a drunken grin.

But it was Cheyenne he saw; Cheyenne whose luminous green gaze widened with hurt.

Damn. Why had she haunted him? Even in Europe? Why did she have this damnable power to lure him? To destroy him?

Cutter kicked a chair out of his way and strode toward her.

Her eyes never left his face even as she whispered to the auctioneer and then began backing away.

"That is impossible, sir," said the auctioneer, signaling to someone behind Cutter.

"Two million then."

Tears sprang into Cheyenne's eyes.

"Sir, this is a respectable gallery. Not a brothel."

Cutter loped up the aisle toward her. "Three million," he yelled.

Shaken, Cheyenne suddenly leapt from the podium and ran.

Cutter vaulted onto the stage after her. "Cheyenne! Wait!"

She looked at him one last time and then dashed wildly out the back door, which slammed so hard the set of rose-spattered china began to shake.

The auctioneer banged his gavel again. "Sold to the gentleman for three million dollars." A pause while the china continued to rattle. "Sir, do you want your china shipped or will you be picking it up this evening yourself?"

With a sweep of his large, brown hand, Cutter raked his arm across the eight place settings of china and sent plates and cups and saucers crashing onto the stage.

There was an instant hush.

"Get him!" a security officer yelled.

Pandemonium broke as armed guards stampeded Cutter.

The guards seized him and hurled him roughly down the stairs off the stage.

As the guards seized him, all he could think of was Cheyenne's pale face as she'd run out the door. Her eyes had been blazing with pain. Tears had spilled down her cheeks as she'd stared at him.

If he had wanted to hurt her and publicly humiliate her, he had ruthlessly succeeded. But he found no pleasure in his success. His behavior tonight was unforgivable.

Loneliness washed over him. As well as regret and self-disgust.

He had been a drunken fool.

Why?

Why hadn't he realized her pain was his?

Three

Cheyenne brushed tears from her burning cheeks as she drove into her circular driveway that was bordered by the tallest magnolia and oak trees in the city. Acres and acres of sweeping green lawn and huge, pink-blossomed azalea hedges that had grown to magical heights encircled and dwarfed the house even though it was a mansion of vast proportions.

Not since her childhood had Cheyenne ever felt so humiliated. *Wrong.* Not since Cutter had seduced her and abandoned her as if she were trash that had washed up on the beach, had she felt so unwanted and unloved. She had worked so hard, learned so much to get past her early life and those hurts.

But where had it all gotten her?

Cutter was as cynical and incapable of love as ever. His opinion of her was as poor as ever. He had even less respect for her than the citizens of Westville had when she had been a child. Still, he would stalk her until she surrendered and gave him what he wanted.

He really believed her to be so low she would sell herself. She remembered how stern and dark his face had been tonight as he'd insulted her in front of all those people.

Confusing emotions tore her.

He had been fierce but wonderful on the island when he'd broken the glass and made love to her. She had loved him. She had carried his child. But he had abandoned her, and she'd been forced to make a terrible marriage.

He was Jeremy's father. Because of Jeremy, he wanted her now. And she...

No. Dear God. No. Not after...

Cutter was cold and hateful.

Her free-spirited mother, for all that the world had despised her, had never slept once, not once, with a man she hadn't wanted.

Cheyenne would not be trapped into marrying another man she didn't love, a man who neither loved her nor respected her, a man who would take her in his arms and seduce her with vengeance in his heart as he had before.

She had to defy him.

But she was as scared of Cutter as Martin had been. Indeed, it had been her empathy for Martin's fear of his brother that had drawn her to Martin in the first place on that fateful afternoon when he'd stood under that gigantic purple wisteria in Sorrento, Italy, that she'd been trying to photograph. She'd asked him to move; he'd agreed but only if she'd join him for a drink. After he'd photographed her with the flowers, he'd told her about Cutter.

Maybe because of her own experience with Chantal, or maybe because the wisteria blossoms had darkened, and she'd taken it as a sign, or maybe it had been because Martin had warmed so passionately to the subject of his hateful brother that Cheyenne had empathized.

Cutter had proved himself to be even worse than Martin had led her to believe. She had thought "Lyon" a good person because the primroses and morning glories had bloomed out of season when she'd first seen him on the beach. But the signals had proved as false as the love he'd professed after he'd seduced her. Cutter had been out to destroy her chances with Martin.

Only Cutter had never considered pregnancy, nor the lengths to which she might go to protect her unborn child from the taint of illegitimacy. Nor had he realized how much Martin might want revenge.

When Martin had discovered she was pregnant, he had seen a way to spite Cutter by claiming something of his brother's. She had married Martin to give her baby the Lord name, which should have been his.

Still, Cutter had ruined all their lives.

The marriage of convenience had been a tragic mistake.

She felt numb from the long years of marital misery. Numb from the new dangers threatening Jeremy.

But whatever she did, she couldn't surrender to Cutter.

For seven years he had cast a long shadow over her life. No more.

She had to get free of him.

No matter what it cost her.

As she drew closer to the dark house, her tears and thoughts of Cutter ceased as a vague new apprehension mushroomed.

The house was shrouded in darkness.

The only light seemed to come from the base of the huge magnolia tree. All the blossoms that had bloomed earlier that evening had withered and fallen to the ground where they gleamed eerily in the moonlight.

The house was dark. Really dark.

Why weren't the lights on?

Ghostly and white in the moonlight, the two-story mansion loomed like a sepulcher from the end of the driveway. Her heartbeat thudded against her rib cage as she drove slowly past the magnolia tree standing in its pool of dead blossoms.

She should never have let Jeremy go home early with Kurt.

No. She mustn't panic. Not yet.

But her heart wouldn't stop skittering as she drove toward the house.

Her stomach knotted.

Why was she suddenly remembering that other night all those months ago when the last flower had fallen from the giant magnolia tree and those two granite-faced Houston detectives had knocked on her door and said, "Mrs. Lord, I'm afraid we've found your husband—"

The outside walls of the mansion were always lit by brilliant floodlights. As were the thick trunks of the trees and the sprawling lawn. The upstairs lights inside the house should be blazing, too. She had been very careful about the lights and the alarm ever since Martin's death.

She knew—even before she shoved the heavy car door open and inhaled the damp, sickly, magnolia-scented night air. She ran, her sparkly black heels flying across the slick concrete sidewalk.

The front door was ajar; the security system off.

"Jeremy," she whispered as she peered into the dark house.

Then she screamed his name.

"*Jeremy. Jeremy. Jeremy.*"

His name bounced off the high ceilings and marble floors in the nearly empty rooms.

When she stepped into the black foyer, glass crunched under her heels. She screamed again, jabbing frantically at the wall where the panel of light switches were.

She found the buttons and jammed her fists against them hard.

The foyer, which contained only a piece or two of essential furniture, burst into light.

"Oh, my God—"

For a moment Cheyenne felt she was in a stranger's house.

There had been a struggle. A Tiffany lamp lay smashed on the checkerboard, black-and-marble floor. Slivers of a crystal Waterford vase glimmered darkly beside spilled red roses and a puddle of water. The corner of her only remaining Aubusson rug was kicked up and smeared with blood.

Beneath the light switches, on the marble top of a Louis XV table, lay a curling, bloodstained paper. A message had been fashioned out of crude newspaper block letters.

Cheyenne froze. Then she dabbed at a spot of blood on the note and began methodically ironing the paper flat on the cold marble with clammy fingertips.

"$5,000,000. No cops."

When she dropped the paper, blood stuck to her hands.

Outside a high wind blew through the trees, snapped huge branches as if they were twigs, tore off roof shingles and shredded pink azalea blossoms.

"Jeremy!"

His name whirled through the house as flowers and roof shingles whirled against the windowpanes.

Cheyenne ran toward the staircase. "Jeremy! Kurt! Mrs. Perkins!"

Where were they?

She heard a faint sound from the basement and rushed to the kitchen where the door to the basement yawned into blackness.

When something alive and warm rubbed her foot, Cheyenne jumped as high as if she'd been bitten by one of her mother's weird night roaming adders.

"Meow!"

A shudder of relief swept her. It was only Panther, Jeremy's black Persian, glaring up at her with flattened ears and suspicious yellow eyes.

Cheyenne turned on the basement light.

"Jeremy?"

In the gloom near the bottom stair lay Kurt and Mrs. Perkins, their hands and feet bound with wire, their mouths plastered with silver duct tape.

Cheyenne rushed down and ripped the tape from their mouths. She untied them and made sure they were still breathing.

Outside the roaring wind made more roof shingles whirl.

"Jeremy? Where's Jeremy?"

Gently she slapped Mrs. Perkins's wrinkled cheek. She shook Kurt's huge shoulders.

No answer. From either of them. Their faces remained slack-jawed, their bodies limp.

She would have to see about them later.

First—she had to find Jeremy.

The mansion was a mock, nineteenth-century French château, with nineteen-foot carved ceilings. Pretentiously tall windows looked out onto her opulent and magical garden. There were arched doorways, ten bedrooms and six bathrooms.

Martin had bought the mansion to impress Cutter and Houston society. Tonight the empty shell seemed a stranger's house. Vaguely she wondered if it had ever been the house of sunshine and warmth and huge flowers, of laughter and parties that had been described in the social columns? Had she really ever loved reading about herself in those columns the next day, which was invariably a degree or two hotter after one of her parties? Had she really ever cared whether people admired her beauty, her success, her child and her marriage?

Had she ever been the happy, assured hostess, wearer of designer gowns, caterer to the rich and famous who had been known for her magical flair with food? Martin the polished host? Had anyone who'd read those columns ever suspected the sinister secrets behind the glitter?

She had been the poor girl, ashamed of her bizarre upbringing, determined to make good and appear normal. She had wanted to be a jet-setting princess—a cultured woman who was glamorous and beautiful and envied. Martin had wanted to be as successful as his brother. Were those ambitions really so wrong?

Like a bewildered and terrified child, Cheyenne ran through the immense shadowy kitchen, down the long, dark hallways, and then up the swirling marble stairway. Turning on every light, she ran from blazing room to room on the second floor, calling Jeremy's name.

As if light and sound or her son's name could banish the dark fear in her heart.

The last bedroom was his. As she approached it, she could see the tall magnolia tree through the hall window and all its gleaming dead blossoms on the lawn.

Jeremy's door was open.

As she had taken nothing from his room to be sold at the auction, all his furnishings were intact.

She stepped inside slowly.

There had been a violent struggle.

His designer sheets had been torn off the bed and dragged halfway across the polished, hardwood floors to the door. His pillows were all over the antique Persian rugs. So were his toys. Encyclopedias littered the floor. There was a smear of blood on the exposed mattress of his four-poster bed.

Like a windup doll moving robotically forward, she took one step after the other toward the empty bed, as if it were a place of undreamed-of evil. Then she sank silently to the faded carpet and leaned against the bed. Tears brimmed in her eyes as she scooped up the pieces of Jeremy's oldest, dearest teddy bear, the one he still slept with and affectionately called Molly Pooh. As Cheyenne lifted it, the severed head, which had been hanging by a thread, fell off. A handful of stuffing exploded in white puffs from the opening and fell around the room as the magnolia blossoms had fluttered to the lawn.

Hysteria bubbled in her throat. She began to scream and brush the pieces of fluff off her black sweater. She was still screaming when the telephone rang jarringly.

Clutching the bear's body, she crawled to the phone. She had Caller ID, so she let it ring a second time.

The digital window read, "No data sent."

She picked up the phone.

"It took you long enough to get home, bitch."

No, dear God. Not that eerie, scratchy voice.

She wept silently. *"Where's Jeremy?"*

"Say hi, Jerry-O."

"M-mommy!" Jeremy shrieked. Jeremy, her miniature daredevil, the bravest, and most adult-seeming little boy in the whole world, was sobbing so hard she could barely understand him. "I tried to climb the magnolia tree, but he has a big knife. H-he cut me. M-m-o-om—"

"My turn, Jerry-O. Mrs. Lord—no cops. Or no more Jerry-O—"

In the background Jeremy screamed.

"Don't you hurt him! Don't you dare hurt him!"

"Now—that depends on you."

The caller hissed instructions and threats.

Jeremy gave a final scream. *"Mommy—"*

When the line went dead, she began to shake and sob violently.

The monster wanted five million dollars. He might as well have asked for the sun and the moon.

She didn't have it.

In her panic she couldn't think of anyone who did. Never had she felt so helpless with fear and so absolutely alone.

Then she remembered Cutter and his drunken bid for her at the auction.

Dear God.

She went to the window. She could see the topmost branches of her huge magnolia tree.

As she stared at the tree, the strange wind died, and a single, gigantic magnolia blossom at the very top, like a star on a Christmas tree, burst into bloom.

It was a sign.

She picked up the phone.

Four

The phone was ringing when Cutter, still in a mood of self-loathing, strode angrily into his enormous penthouse suite at the Warwick. He was carrying a single Wedgwood cup fashioned of pink roses—all that was left of the smashed china set that he had been forced to buy for an exorbitant price.

Because *she* loved flowers, dozens of yellow tulips in silver vases emblazoned the four bedrooms and the beautiful living room of the suite. Two balconies overlooked the city. Potted geraniums now decorated them, too.

The suite had been stocked with whiskey and champagne and a dozen other silly romantic items. There was a filmy black negligee lying across his king-size bed in his master bedroom. Perfumed bath oils lined his immense marble tub. A stack of CDs of romantic music lay beside a player. There was even a pile of lurid paperbacks on the bedside table to tempt a lady of dubious literary tastes.

Foolishly, arrogantly he had believed that tonight would be the night Cheyenne would share his suite and his bed.

He focused on a single pink china rose on the fragile china cup.

No way. Not after what he'd done.

Once again he had made a grave miscalculation where the troublesome Cheyenne Rose was concerned.

He remembered the day she had come to him and begged him to help Martin. She had been so beautiful with that rose in her hair. Too beautiful in her prim white suit with her red hair drawn back from her face in that ridiculously tight chignon. Except for the flower, by wearing no makeup and excessively tailored clothes, she had done everything possible to erase her sexuality. Yet she had fired his blood as never before.

As she'd sat in his office he had remembered her naked on the island with flowers in her hair. He had remembered touching her breasts and thighs with his lips and tongue. He had remembered the guttural whimpers that had risen from her throat. He had remembered all the equally sexual things she had done to arouse him. He had remembered how incredibly tender and sweet and wild she was. Last of all, he had remembered sharing the secrets of his soul with her, and he'd felt grim and frightened at the thought that he might still be genuinely in love with her. It was then that the thought of Martin possessing her for all those years had driven Cutter so mad with jealousy that he'd propositioned her by undoing the buttons of her jacket and touching her, saying he'd help her—for a price.

When she'd tried to run, he'd grabbed her hand and yanked her closer, aligning her body to his for a second or two. She had struggled, and as always she had felt hot. So hot. So incredibly hot, and yet so soft and dark and mysterious. His fury had heightened his lust; he had wanted her then more than he had ever wanted a woman. He had seen his own savage desire reflected in her angry eyes.

She had said very softly, almost sobbing, "You just don't get it, do you? I am not for sale. That's not why I married your brother. That's not why I came to you."

He'd let her go.

With trembling fingers she'd tried to refasten her jacket. Then she'd run.

He hadn't believed her then.

He wasn't so sure now.

So—why *had* she married Martin?

Damn.

He would ask her. Not that she'd tell him.

It had taken him a month or so to realize he'd treated her abysmally and feel ashamed. He would have to stop bullying her the way he bullied his business subordinates.

Tonight he had let liquor and his temper get the best of him again. After tonight, convincing her she had no choice other than him was going to take much longer than he'd originally expected.

The phone kept ringing.

He was tired.

Too tired to dwell on his remorse about her or talk business to one of his vice presidents on the other side of the world.

He needed a drink. Then a shower. Then sleep. After the stunt he'd pulled at the auction, it was a miracle he wasn't spending tonight in jail.

The caller could go to hell.

Cutter stepped out onto the balcony and gazed at the sliver of moon in the starless sky and then at the blaze of the city spread out before him and at the cars flying beneath in the dark, the fire of their lights flashing brighter than diamonds and rubies.

The beauty of the night did nothing for him. He had never given a damn for pretty views, and tonight this particular view depressed him. Perhaps there was some emptiness inside him, some secret flaw in his psyche that prevented a response. He saw a city filled with more than a million people, and he hated the sight of it because it only made him feel his own isolation more fiercely.

People said he was incapable of love. Maybe they were right.

Again he saw Cheyenne's pale face and her tear-glazed

eyes and felt swamped by guilt. He drew a harsh breath. In the bar he had wanted her more than ever, but she had rejected him.

He left the balcony for the kitchen where he splashed whiskey into her ridiculous cup made of roses.

Finally when the phone wouldn't quit, he grabbed it and barked, "Cutter Lord here."

Hysterical sobs. A shrill cry of anguish that cut all the way to his soul.

He slammed the cup down on the stove so hard he damn near broke it.

"Cutter! Thank God! I—I thought you weren't ever going to answer!"

A woman was sobbing so incoherently he could neither understand her nor identify her.

His heart began to beat very fast. "Who is this?"

All she could do was repeat his name. *"Cutter! Cutter...."*

"Cheyenne?" he whispered, his low voice becoming tense and yet uncustomarily gentle. "Cheyenne?"

"Yes. Yes," she rasped.

Then she dropped the phone.

"Damn." Her terror shook him as he waited while she fumbled to pick it up.

"Cutter—! Are you still there?"

"I'm here." His voice was calm.

She was breathing fast, way too fast.

"Honey, take a couple of deep breaths and then tell me what's wrong."

But he knew. Before she said a single word, he felt as if a fist had slammed viciously into his chest and was gripping his heart in a stranglehold.

"They took him! They took Jeremy."

The fist tightened like talons. This was his fault. He had known the danger she and Jeremy were in. He should have forced her to accept his terms. "Who?"

"I don't know. Maybe whoever murdered Martin."

He knew who Martin's killer was. And how dangerous he was.

"Cutter, you have to help me. Please. There's no one else I can turn to. I'll do anything, everything you want, sleep with you, marry you—if only you'll—"

So—he had found her price.

But it wasn't money. Or marriage. It was the life of their son.

He felt more disgusted with himself than ever.

None of that mattered now. "Stay where you are," he growled. "I'll get over there as fast as I can."

Cheyenne went down to see about Kurt and Mrs. Perkins. They were still lying in the exact positions she had left them with their eyes closed. This time she saw the half-open bottle of sleeping pills on the floor beside Kurt. Most of the pills were in the cap and the bottle. Which meant they hadn't taken them all. Still—

Cheyenne felt their wrists.

Their pulses were strong.

She began slapping them lightly on their faces and shouting their names.

Kurt groaned and lashed at her drunkenly.

"Don't take him," Mrs. Perkins moaned, her words slow and uncustomarily thick. "He's just a little boy. Please don't take him. Please don't kill him."

Cheyenne sank to the floor beside them in despair.

"Where is he, Mrs. Perkins? Where is he?"

"Cheyenne!"

She heard Cutter's running footsteps.

Dimly she was aware of Cutter bursting into the brilliantly lit mansion like a volcano.

"Cheyenne!" Cutter's voice boomed everywhere, echoing in the cold, empty house.

She got up slowly, listlessly. The bottle of pills fell from her hand and rolled across the concrete floor. Panther meowed and raced excitedly up the stairs ahead of her.

She followed, careful not to trip over the cat. Dazed, she almost ran into Cutter in the hall.

He took her into his arms and crushed her against his hard chest. He was strong, yet he cradled her to him very gently. He cupped her delicate chin in his huge hands and smoothed her hair out of her eyes. "It's going to be okay," he whispered.

She was stunned by such tenderness from him. Gone was the crude brother-in-law who'd tried to undress her in his office. Gone, too, was the fierce, dark stranger who had bid for her at the auction. In his place was the lover who had captured her heart on the island and had become the father of her only child. The man who had made love to her first and then bared his soul.

Hungrily she drank in his words.

"I'll find him. I swear I will. But you've got to help me, Cheyenne. You've got to pull yourself together. I can't do it without you."

Very gently, with his hand at the back of her waist, he guided her into the kitchen. "Honey, I'm going to make a pot of coffee while you tell me everything. Absolutely everything."

He was at the stove when she foolishly threw herself into his arms again and began weeping inconsolably. "He's gone. And it's all my fault. I should never have left him alone. It's no use."

"You've got to stop it," Cutter ordered, petting her hair. "Please...stop. I can't bear it if you cry now, Cheyenne. You can cry later, if—"

His voice broke.

She stared at him in horror, understanding his allusion.

Then something outside her fear and their distrust took charge and made mockery of all the years of hurt and anger and despair. They clung to each other hungrily, each as desperate as the other. Each understanding perfectly how the other felt.

Their loss bound them. He was hurt and afraid—as she was. In their mutual need to console and comfort and soothe the other, everything that had stood between them melted away. She felt shattered inside, and so did he. And yet because he was there, she could bear it because in that moment she felt that more, far more than just her son bound her to this man she had never been able to forget or forgive.

She closed her eyes when she felt him begin to shake helplessly.

"It's my fault, too," he said abruptly, breaking the spell, letting her go, almost pushing her away. "But we can think about that later. We've got work to do now."

"Yes... Yes," she agreed dully, sinking into a kitchen chair, feeling strangely bereft and more afraid without his hard arms around her.

Outside—the night was totally dark.

Jeremy needed to pee real bad, but he was afraid to ask Baldy if he could go.

"I'll be Mr. X to you, and you'll be Jerry-O to me," the kidnapper had whispered in the pirogue as he poled through dark water carpeted with water hyacinths.

Baldy was great big. He had the ugly bald head of a yucky toad and the thick body of a wrestler. He wore wire-rimmed sunglasses even in the swamp. His fatigues smelled as yucky as the dead, rotting smells that seeped up through the hyacinths.

Jeremy was used to adults being impressed with him 'cause he was smart and pretended to act brave. He wanted to act big. To pretend he knew all the answers. To be unafraid. But everything about Baldy sent chills down Jeremy's spine.

Tears leaked behind Jeremy's eyelids all the time now. They were in a shack in the swamp, and as Jeremy stood tensely on a rickety wooden chair in front of a blackened mirror, Baldy held his knife so close to his face, the blade got all blurry. Suddenly Baldy heard what he thought was a motor. He snapped the blade shut and tiptoed to the door.

Outside there were only birdcalls, liquid ploppings in the pea-soup water and the hum of giant mosquitoes.

Jeremy's bladder felt like it was about to pop.

He wished he were home with his mother. The mere thought of her tenderness and gentleness, of the way she would hold him if he were scared or kiss him if he were hurt brought more tears and then total loss of control.

Suddenly it was all too much.

Three things happened at once.

He wet his pants like a baby.

He screamed as the warm urine trickled down his legs.

Then he bolted for the trees.

If he could be fast enough— And climb high enough—

But even though he raced at top speed, it was as if he moved in slow motion.

Baldy was that much faster.

"You're going to be sorry, Jerry-O."

A large hand gripped his collar in a stranglehold. Then the knife handle slammed into Jeremy's head, and the cabin exploded in tiny red dots.

Cheyenne was tired. So tired. And yet too restless to sleep. She'd wanted to go out and look for Jeremy with Cutter and his men, but Cutter had said she had to stay by the phone in case the kidnapper called back.

For once she'd obeyed him without a quarrel. After she'd told him everything she knew, he'd interviewed Mrs. Perkins and Kurt. Then he'd made dozens of calls to people on both sides of the border, calls he hadn't allowed her to listen to. When two of his men had shown up to guard her, he'd gone out without telling her where he was going.

"Cutter, I want to know everything," she had begged.

They had looked at each other for a long moment. He hadn't trusted her any more than she trusted him.

"Yes," he said at last. "Yes. But in this case, the less you know the better."

"Why?"

"Martin was involved with some very dangerous people."

"No kidding."

Cutter had stared at her.

"Do you know who they are?" she asked.

"Do you?"

"Martin never told me anything."

That statement revealed too much about their marriage.

Cutter's face darkened with grim sympathy. Tenderly he kissed her brow. "I have to go."

"Tell me who— Tell me where you're—"

"Shh! Paul's here, if you need him."

"I need *you*."

"I never thought I'd hear you say that," Cutter said gently. "You warm my heart."

"How can you joke?"

He took a long breath. "I'm not joking."

"When will you be back?"

"Look—" Again, his voice was gentle.

Cutter opened the door, and she felt the vastness of the chasm between them.

"I will go crazy here with nothing to do. Without you."

"We've been through this. You must wait by the phone."

When she'd nodded, calmer for an instant, he'd left before she grew hysterical again.

So, now, here she was—in her bedroom, the bedroom that she'd filled with antiques, the pink bedroom that had always been hers alone, and never Martin's. Tonight, denuded of its best furniture, without Cutter, the room felt every bit as much of a prison as it had all those years of her unendurable marriage.

She lay down on her bed to wait. Odd, how she longed for Cutter's return. He had been so kind. So concerned. So helpful. Not blaming her at all even when she'd professed her guilt again and again.

He had taken her into his arms and said repeatedly, "No, it's my fault more than it's yours. I was blind to what you and Martin were going through. But after you came to see me that day when you asked me to help Martin, I investigated Martin's operation. Since then, and since his death, I have learned a great deal about the people he was doing business with. I know how dangerous they are.''

If he knew who they were, why was it so hard to find their son? Why did he have all his men scouring the city and state for Jeremy? Why were his top executives from all over the world flying in tomorrow morning to help with the search? Why had he told his pilot to load his jet with rifles and high-capacity assault weapons? With hundreds of rounds of hollow grade ammunition, and extra clips? With pump shotguns, and side arms? When she'd asked, Cutter had refused to answer, infuriating her by insisting that the less she knew the better.

''But why do you need guns?''

''You don't want to know,'' he'd said.

''If Jeremy gets hurt, I'll never forgive you.''

''Another crime to add to your long list.'' His skin had gone gray, his eyes bleak. ''Honey, do you think I'd ever forgive myself?''

''I'm sorry I said that,'' she had whispered then, feeling his pain in all its intensity because it was hers.

Again she felt bound to him, as she'd felt on the island, as she'd felt through all the years of her unhappy marriage to his brother. Again, everything melted away but their need for each other as two human beings sharing a terrible crisis.

''I'm sorry for belittling you at the auction,'' he whispered.

She put her hand very gently over his. ''Maybe... No. Not maybe. I should have been nicer to you, too. Maybe it's time we started giving each other the benefit of the doubt—''

They had looked at each other in a new way, and yet in the old way, too.

''Sounds good to me,'' he had said, cupping her chin. ''Be strong. I need to know you believe in me.''

Then he had left her.

She lay in the darkness, her mind spinning crazily with cherished memories and nightmarish visions. She remembered the day Jeremy had been born. She had nearly died, and Martin hadn't cared. The pain had been terrible, and she had lost control and screamed and screamed for Cutter. Then days later when he'd come, she'd let Martin throw him out even though she had longed for Cutter to stay forever.

She remembered Jeremy cutting his first tooth, saying his first words, taking his first steps, climbing his first tree, falling out of a tree and breaking his arm—his first broken bone. He had been reading books at three and doing multiplication tables, too. He had always tried so hard to do everything well and had passed out of two grades. Martin, who'd rarely noticed him, had despised his son's accomplishments because they reminded him of Cutter's. For the same reason he had disliked Jeremy's avidly curious nature and his tendency to snoop and eavesdrop.

Cutter who might have felt pride in his son, had never been there for any of the *first* events in his son's life. Maybe now, Cutter would never know Jeremy.

Was Jeremy even still alive? She kept hearing his final scream before the kidnapper had hung up. Hours later she was still awake when Cutter, his dark face even grimmer and more haggard, returned alone.

"Jeremy?" she whispered, pushing herself up by the elbows when Cutter came and sat wearily in the chair by her bed and turned on a lamp.

Golden light spilled over them both and shone in his black hair. The shadows under his tired eyes were as dark as those moon-shaped circles under hers. For no reason at all she felt again that vague urge to touch him, to stroke his hair soothingly, to fling herself in his arms and seek her own comfort. But some other part of herself was determined to reject him.

"Nothing yet," he told her. He picked up one of her paperbacks on the table and thumbed through it with a grim smile. "How can you like this junk?"

"For the happy endings," she whispered.

He was silent.

"Any progress at all?" she asked.

His face was unreadable as he set her book down. His voice was clipped when he leaned closer. "I told you— don't ask. False hopes are too painful. For both of us. I'll tell you when I know something."

Her mouth thinned when Cutter got up from the chair.

She ached for him to stay near her. She distrusted this closeness she felt toward him since she'd decided long ago that he had to be the coldest man on earth.

"So—any calls?" he demanded.

Wearily she shook her head.

He went into her bathroom and turned on the water.

Feeling abandoned, she called after him, "What are you doing?"

When he didn't answer she couldn't bear the room without him, so she arose and trailed after him as if she were a lonesome puppy.

He was sitting on the side of her tub, steam billowing around him in perfumed plumes, as he tested the hot water with his hand.

His kind smile made her feel warm and safe and long to be in his arms.

"You're worn-out. If you can't sleep, you can at least take a bath," he said, his voice concerned.

"No—"

Outside the sky was streaked with red. The sun was coming up. She saw a new bud on the magnolia tree.

"It's nearly six," he said. "It's going to be a long day. You're going to take a hot bath. When you're through, you're going to come downstairs and I'll cook us both some breakfast."

She protested even though she liked his protective treatment and kindnesses. "I'm not hungry. I'm not—"

And yet, she wanted all these things from him. And more.

"I know. Neither am I. We're both going to eat anyway. Then we'll go outside and walk in your garden. You can tell me about Jeremy's daredevil, tree-climbing adventures.''

With Jeremy gone, she shouldn't care about bathing or eating or talking or being with Cutter or about anything, but because Cutter wanted her to, she did those things and felt stronger. Because he was with her, she didn't feel so alone.

Because he shared her burden and, thereby, lightened it, she almost felt—*hope*.

Later, when neither of them could sleep but both of them were even more exhausted, he drew her down on the couch in the library beside him where they both tried to read— he a business magazine, she a trashy thriller. But it wasn't long before she found her eyelids drooping. She laid her head back against the couch, thinking to rest her eyes.

Some time during the night she awoke and was startled to realize she had been dreaming of Cutter. She was even more startled to find her body was nestled intimately into his. Her head lay upon his shoulder. Her splayed fingers fanned out over his thigh. His arm lay burningly across her breast.

They had slept together as trustingly and as contentedly as they had on the island. Yet now the knowledge of it made her skin grow hot and her breath come raspily. When she grew rigidly still, not daring to move, lest she wake him, he intuitively sensed the change in her and drowsily opened his eyes.

"Cheyenne?" he whispered softly, solemnly. "Are you still here, my darling?"

Darling?

He had called her his darling.

She jumped at the gentleness of his husky voice, intending to run.

But he held her there in the soft, hot darkness.

Not with his hands or by any use of force. Not even with more huskily spoken words. His stark gaze was enough to make her know how much he needed her.

If he wanted her that much, she wanted to stay.

She wanted to go on lying with him.

And for a long time they did continue to lie together in the darkness, their legs and arms tangled, neither of them daring to speak again or bat so much as an eyelash for fear of frightening the other away.

At last he stirred, and she felt his warm hand brush her brow.

She lifted her face against his fingers and closed her eyes like a contented cat as he stroked her.

He brushed his lips against her hair, his breath burning into her scalp. Then his mouth stole lower across her face, bestowing tingly, feathery kisses upon each closed eyelid. She held her breath as his mouth slowly trailed down her velvet cheek to her lips.

He kissed her very slowly, making her wait until she felt so hot she ached.

At the same time she willed herself not to feel anything as he kissed her and caressed her. Not when Jeremy—

And yet, when Cutter's lips touched hers, her fear lessened, and an entirely different kind of emotion flamed inside her.

Suddenly she wanted to touch Cutter, to hold him, to taste him. She opened her lips so his tongue could enter and become one with the warm recesses of her mouth.

Desire for him wound her tighter.

And yet—

He positioned himself over her, fumbling to undo his slacks and her clothes, too. In the next instant she felt his hot naked skin against her own.

Then he was urging her thighs apart, and she felt his body pressing toward the very center of her being.

Her own breathing was as harsh and irregular as his. Her fingers were clutching his upper arms, pulling him closer. She wanted him. So much. She was afraid of the dark. Of feeling alone. Of being scared and going through this nightmarish time without him. She loved—

No. No.

This wasn't love. This was terror and need. She was all mixed up.

How could she be doing this?

Feeling this?

With him?

Now?

"What are you so afraid of?" he demanded, stopping his kisses, and drawing back, his voice rough and harshly constricted with sharp sexual need.

He had asked her what she was so afraid of.

You. This. Everything.

An uncontrollable shudder went through her. But she couldn't say the words.

Still, he knew and understood.

His mood softened. "Hey, it's okay," he whispered.

No! It's not!

"It's okay," he repeated.

She squeezed her eyes shut again, not wanting to look at him as he levered his body away from hers and allowed her to disentangle her legs from his.

Blindly she pushed herself off him. Then, clasping her clothes around her body, she ran.

And yet when she had found the safety and solitude of her own room, she found no peace without him. If anything the pulse in her throat beat more wildly.

As she tore off her wrinkled clothes, showered and put on fresh ones, she thought how different it was having Cutter in the house rather than Martin. Even as she regretted what had nearly happened between them and feared that it would happen again, Cutter seemed to belong with her as Martin had never belonged. In all the years of her marriage there had never been one shared moment between herself and Martin. Not one moment when they had cared the same way about the same thing.

There had never been shameless desire, either.

Cutter mattered to her, more than she wanted him to. In this terrible hour, Cutter cared as intensely as she did about finding their son. And he was the only person on earth who

did. Maybe she didn't agree with his methods, but his tenderness and thoughtfulness and protectiveness, even his se-
ductiveness, had touched her deeply.

She knew he was cutting through all her carefully constructed defenses far too easily. Still, because of Cutter,
whom she had wanted to hate all these years, she could
hold on to her sanity even though she knew that when this
was over, no matter what happened—Cutter would win.

Which meant she would lose.

And yet... Now, during this dreadful time, there was no
one else she wanted to be with except him.

Her feelings for him were dangerous.

Too dangerous.

She had wanted him inside her.

She still did.

She wanted him with all her heart.

He knew it.

And he would use it.

Five

Cutter Lord had learned the hard way it wasn't smart to play fair with criminals.

Cutter knew who had taken Jeremy. A great many people knew.

But when Cutter's men hit the street and started asking questions, nobody talked.

As the long hours of the second day ticked by, and the deadline to pay the ransom drew closer, Cutter knew he had to find another way.

He had done business in dangerous countries all over the world for more than a decade. He had been held up before.

It was bad business to pay ransoms. In South America standard operating procedure among kidnappers was to take the money and kill the victim and, thus, eliminate the chance for identification.

Cutter had paid a ransom once. Big mistake. So huge Cutter had vowed never to pay a ransom again.

Not that he'd told Cheyenne. She didn't trust him, and she was too naive to understand the reasons behind his tactics. She wouldn't cooperate.

If Cutter couldn't find Jeremy soon, Cutter had decided to counterattack.

He'd up the ante and make the bastard sweat, too.

As an international businessman, Cutter knew that international borders were less precise than the neat black lines drawn on maps. Cultures and morals and laws overlapped.

Men who knew how to play the laws of bordering nations against each other could get rich as could men who knew how to satisfy the illegal lusts and unmet financial needs of their neighbors.

Rich men such as these grew very powerful. So powerful they bought lawmakers and became gods who believed themselves above the laws of any land.

José Hernando was such a man and such a lawless god. On his vast ranches in northern Mexico, he bred the finest bulls in the world for the most famous matadors. Hernando spoke three languages, drove race cars in Europe and made love to beautiful movie stars and opera singers. It was said that when he was done with a woman, he always granted her her most heartfelt wish. In his quieter moments he hunted big game or played chess with his nephews and his only daughter.

José was richer and more powerful than many presidents. He bought and sold American politicians, ambassadors, cardinals and, of course, women. Not only did he make millions in his legitimate businesses such as ranching, banking, telecommunications and real estate, he made even more illegally.

As a result Hernando had cash to launder. He had a keen interest in struggling businessmen on both sides of the border. Which is how he had come to invest in Martin's failing properties.

Through his investigations into Martin's affairs, Cutter had learned that José had become Martin's partner after Martin's much-publicized meteoric rise to wealth. Martin's businesses had grown too fast; he'd acquired too much credit and lived too high. Then the Texas economy had taken a dip. He'd skipped payments to his bankers; he would have lost everything had Hernando not poured dirty money into Martin's vacant apartment complexes and office buildings. Large sums of cash had also been dumped into his import-export business.

All had gone well until Martin had begun to skim. Hernando had cut him off and demanded payment. So had his bankers. That was when Martin had begged Cutter to release his hold on his private fortune.

Cutter had refused. When he'd discovered that Martin's life was at stake, it had been too late.

Cutter would never forgive himself for stalling. It was partly his fault that Martin was dead, and Hernando had Jeremy.

Guilt and bitterness and jealousy and all the other dark emotions Cutter had buried on that sweltering afternoon nearly seven years ago in an Indonesian jungle when he'd learned of Martin's and Cheyenne's betrayal suddenly threatened to overwhelm him.

Cutter had left Cheyenne's bed on Lord Island to jog on the beach, only to find Paul O'Connor and several men who'd just arrived by boat on the Lord dock. They had brought news of a refinery fire in Malaysia and had told Cutter he had to leave immediately for Singapore. There hadn't been time to say goodbye to Cheyenne.

Martin had been waiting for him at the airport. He hadn't seemed at all upset to learn that Cutter wanted to marry Cheyenne. He had even shaken Cutter's hand.

Leaving Martin in charge, Cutter had boarded his jet. But when he'd gotten to Singapore and called home, he'd been unable to reach Cheyenne. He'd asked Martin to find her.

Martin hadn't called back for several weeks. Finally when he did call on that steamy afternoon, Cutter had been exhausted from working day and night with the dead and dying of the refinery explosion.

The jungle heat had been fierce, and Cutter hadn't slept for three days. Martin had sounded jaunty and well rested.

"So—did you find Cheyenne?" Cutter had demanded, cutting short the pleasantries.

There had been an awkward pause. "Yes."

"Well?"

"She and I are getting married...."

"What—"

"And, for once, there isn't a damn thing you can do about it."

"What the hell are you—"

"She was *my* girl. Not yours. And I'm marrying her."

"You're what?"

"All our lives, you were the genius. You pushed me around. You controlled the family, the business, our parents, my money, my women—everything. You always set me up to take the fall and made me look like I was a failure."

"Get back to Cheyenne—"

"She's marrying *me* Saturday. I'd ask you to be best man, but, there's no way in hell you can get back in two days."

"I'll be there."

Cutter had walked out on his Malaysian responsibilities to try to get home in time to stop the wedding.

The ensuing lawsuits had nearly destroyed Lord Enterprise. And for what?

Martin had beaten him up at the wedding. Cheyenne had coldly rejected him. Not once had she come to see him in the hospital. Cutter had fired Martin and seized control of his money. According to their father's will, Cutter had had the right to act as he had. Still, Cutter might have relented if he hadn't gone ballistic after he'd seen Jeremy in the hospital and realized Martin had taken his son.

A case could be made that it was Cutter's fault Jeremy had been kidnapped. Martin would never have had to borrow money if Cutter hadn't seized his fortune.

Hell.

Nobody could change the past. It was better to bury it and deal with the present.

Cutter had lived all over the world—in primitive countries with primitive cultures. His experiences had changed him, hardened him. He was no longer the sophisticated, law-abiding citizen of the United States a great many less-than-insightful people who had known him for years thought him to be.

Cutter believed in a more primitive code of honor than that currently fashionable in the United States. An eye for an eye. A tooth for a tooth.

It was time somebody taught José Hernando a lesson.

It would mean crossing the line as far as U.S. laws were concerned. Maybe even as far as his own conscience was concerned.

It would mean fighting fire with gasoline.

It would mean making a mortal enemy of the extremely dangerous man.

If his men made the smallest slip, Cutter could be indicted on international conspiracy and kidnapping charges. Still, it was his only chance to get Jeremy back alive.

Though a killer, Hernando was a man of surface geniality and charm. Since his wife's death, he had become a legendary ladies' man.

But he had an Achilles' heel.

There was one person he loved—his beautiful sixteen-year-old daughter who had been born to the only woman Hernando had ever loved enough to marry.

It was said that this angelic girl was an exact look-alike of her beloved mother who had died in childbirth.

Even now Cutter's men were storming the mountain stronghold deep in the interior of Mexico where the girl lived on one of Hernando's ranches under the tightest security.

When Cutter's men telephoned with the news that they had the girl, Cutter would call Hernando and demand Jeremy.

If Cutter's men didn't call, Jeremy would die.

And he, Cutter, would lose not only his son, but Cheyenne. If his men did get the girl, he could end up in jail. Or be murdered by one of Hernando's thugs. Cutter, who prized winning above all things, was very much afraid he couldn't win this one.

He remembered Cheyenne's passionate response to him that morning.

She had been hot and tender.

As sweetly responsive to every nuance of his physical and emotional needs as before.

It wasn't over between them.

He didn't want to lose her.

But he would—if he didn't get Jeremy back.

The temperature hit one hundred degrees. It was a record. Cheyenne was running on raw nerves.

Finding Cutter's dark mood and the house oppressive, she had gone outside to water her garden. Before the kidnapping when she worked in the garden, Jeremy used to follow her. He would play beside her, batting bushes with pointed sticks, pointing out weird bugs. Or he would climb the nearest tree and read a book up there or holler down at her.

Today, no matter how long she aimed her hose at the ground in front of a plant, the earth remained as dry and parched as a desert. She could almost feel the leaves shriveling and turning brown in the fierce, unseasonable heat, and finally, since she knew all this to be a bad sign, her pain and terror became so great she coiled her hose beside a clump of withering day lilies next to the house and went back inside.

The long, hot day wore on until the hour to pay the ransom was almost upon them. Cutter and she had kept to themselves since their lovemaking session—she in her bedroom while Cutter just sat in the library downstairs, his black head in his hands as he waited by the telephone.

Why did he just sit down there—waiting, doing nothing? She could do that. Anybody could.

She glanced at her watch. He had thirty minutes.

Why wouldn't he tell her something?

Or do something? Or order her to do something?

She, who never bit her nails, had torn them to the quick. She was going mad. *Mad.*

The minutes dragged by. Condensation misted the windows. A feeling of suffocation began to close in on her, choking her, filling her with mindless panic. Her throat felt as dry as the dust in her garden. Her fingertips grew numb. She began to breathe at a shallow, rapid pace. Suddenly she couldn't stand it a second longer. Cutter had told her to rest, to stay in her bedroom till he came up to her.

But she couldn't. Not when the pink walls seemed to be closing in on her. Not when Jeremy was in danger and her emotions shrilled at a fever pitch.

The phone rang once and was answered somewhere else in the house.

She sat up on her bed.

Cutter had ordered her to leave him alone in the library. He had ordered her to wait until he came to her.

Who was he to order her about in her own house? When her baby was gone and her garden was dying? When she was desperate and afraid and feeling so alone? When she needed to know everything that was going on? When she needed *him.*

White-faced, she stormed out of her bedroom, down the stairs and into the library.

He didn't look up when she came in.

His broad back was to her. He was sitting in the dark, hunched over the phone as he spoke, and his voice was so low and hard, she shivered. There was a flat, hostile quality in it she had never heard before.

She caught his words very clearly, "You play chess, don't you. I have your queen. So, it's checkmate, *mi amigo.*"

Cutter hung up the phone.

She made a sound and he turned and looked at her.

Then he stood up and stared past her coldly, out the long window to the parched lawn and withering garden and to the driveway as if he hadn't seen her. As if he were indifferent to her presence, he frowned as he watched a squirrel race across the sidewalk and then up a tree.

How could Cutter take the slightest interest in anything other than Jeremy?

She felt the gap of the lost years between them, the gap of this terrible lack of understanding between them.

Who was he? Why had she turned to this cold man, of all people, in her time of crisis?

She saw a tall, well-built, raven-haired man with deep black eyes and a devastatingly handsome, unshaved face. Gone was the gentle lover who had come so close to seducing her. This man was a stranger whose expression was so ruthless she felt chilled.

Still she cried, "Who were you talking to? How can you talk about playing chess—a mere game—when our son's life is at stake? Why don't you do something? Why don't you go out and find him? Why do you just sit here—hour after hour? I could have done that by myself."

"So, is that what you think?" he asked quietly, wearily. Again there was something dead and horrible in his voice. His dark gaze pleaded for something she couldn't put into words.

"I want you to go. I'm sorry I ever called you about Jeremy. I'm sorry…about last night."

He made a frustrated sound deep in his throat. "So am I, honey."

She sucked in a deep, hurt breath, and turned away, embarrassed.

Then the phone rang, increasing their tension.

Cutter seized it instantly. "Yes?"

His face went very gray as he listened.

She hung on that single word that he'd uttered. On the hard expression in his eyes. On the grim set of his mouth.

After a second or two he slammed the phone down.

The silence between them was electric.

"What is it?" she whispered. "Was that him?"

Cutter nodded. "I'm leaving now," he said to her, without anger. Without fear. Without any visible emotion.

And yet...there was a difference in him.

"To pay the ransom? To get Jeremy?"

He hesitated.

"Yes," he finally answered.

"You're lying! I know it!"

Her eyes filled with helpless tears when he picked up his jacket, slung it over his shoulder, and strode silently past her.

She chased after him. "I—I don't believe you! Where are you really going? Is Jeremy dead or alive? What did you do with all those guns? What do you know that you aren't telling me?" She paused. "Tell me! How can you just calmly walk out like—"

He turned, and his eyes were deep and dark and yet faintly sympathetic now.

"I want to go with you!" she cried.

"No. It's too dangerous." He brushed the tip of her nose and then her cheek with his fingertip. In another man it might have been a gesture of affection. "This isn't an easy situation. Trust me," he whispered tightly, his dark face like stone. "Please. Just a little while longer. This is almost over. Jeremy's alive. I won't come back without him. I swear. Trust me."

Trust me? How could she when he had betrayed her before? When somehow she knew he was holding something back?

She threw herself into his arms, and he held her till she quieted.

But even as his touch was a comfort, she felt the coldness in him, the fierce desire to leave her and be on his way.

"Trust me," he whispered and was gone.

Something had gone wrong.

Jeremy shivered in his urine-soaked pajamas. He was bound and gagged, trussed up like a pig for slaughter. His mouth was dry, and it hurt when he swallowed. He stared out the window at a tall cypress tree and wished he was free so he could climb it. No bad guy could ever get him again.

He would never go home again.

Or climb trees.

Or read books.

Or win prizes at school for knowing more stuff than the other kids.

Or see his mother.

Across the room Baldy sat by the phone and stared at him with glimmering, murderous hatred as he mopped beads of sweat from his brow with a dirty gray towel.

What was he waiting for?

They had been in the sweltering shack two days.

Suddenly the cellular phone on the table rang.

The killer laughed when he recognized the caller.

Then his jowls sagged.

A minute later he slammed the phone onto the table and grabbed his knife. The uneven floorboards creaked as he walked heavily toward Jeremy.

The horrible big blade gleamed. Baldy's murderous eyes shone fiercely.

Jeremy clenched his eyelids shut.

He was going to die.

He wanted his mommy.

Mommy—

A tear spilled down his cheek as he wondered if God let little boy angels climb trees up in Heaven.

Six

Cheyenne ran out of the house when she saw Cutter's black limousine in the driveway beneath the shadows of the trees. She didn't notice that the earth was moist or how green the leaves were or that there were more blossoms on her trees and hedges.

She held her breath when the long black car stopped and a back door was flung open.

Then Cutter got out with Jeremy hanging limply in his arms.

"He's going to be all right," Cutter said, smiling grimly when she saw the bruises on her son's throat and cheeks. His voice grew cold and fierce. "But call a doctor."

She touched Jeremy's brow and felt its dangerous coolness. The boy didn't stir. Not even when she kissed him and whispered his name.

Then Cutter's hand closed over hers, his strong fingers entwining with hers.

She held on to him tightly, feeling again that inexplicable bond they shared as together they walked from beneath the dark trees shrouding their driveway toward the brightly lit mansion.

Jeremy was in bed, his face pale, his body still, his arms wrapped tightly around the headless body of Molly Pooh. The doctor had given him a sedative.

Cheyenne watched the rise and fall of Jeremy's thin chest. Usually he was so full of life. So exuberant.

He'd been through a lot.

"He's going to be all right," the doctor assured her after Jeremy shut his eyes and she could no longer see the haunting fear there.

Still, she had lain down beside her son in the narrow bed and wrapped her arms around his wiry body.

"You're safe. You're safe," she whispered.

"Because of Uncle Cutter," he had murmured over and over again like a refrain, including him as if he would belong to them forever, as if already he were a member of their immediate family.

Because of Uncle Cutter.

The refrain was oddly comforting to her, too.

She had lain beside her son, holding him, wanting to be there when he woke up.

She wanted to be there with him always.

She didn't know how she was ever going to let him out of her sight again.

Jeremy awoke in the night and turned to her. Never before had she realized how much he looked like his father. "Can you sew Molly Pooh's head back on?"

"Of course, darling. Of course." She petted his thick black hair.

"Tomorrow?" he queried.

"Now. I'll do it now. While you sleep."

They looked into each other's eyes, and neither could say the things they wanted to say as he handed her the bear's body.

"There's nothing to be afraid of now," she whispered.

He nodded, but she could tell by his wide eyes that he didn't believe her.

"Uncle Cutter said it was okay to be afraid. That I didn't have to feel bad 'cause I was so scared."

"You don't."

She wanted to know everything that had happened to him, but she couldn't ask him. He wanted to tell her, even though he knew he never would because he couldn't bear the memories.

Jeremy's black eyes brightened just a bit. "Is Uncle Cutter still here?"

She nodded bleakly. "Yes, and he has lots of guards here to keep you safe."

"He showed me his gun. He said he'd shoot the bad man if he tried to come back. I want a gun, too. He said I could have one. That he'd teach me to shoot— That—"

"Hush. Hush."

She frowned, not wanting to think of guns or the implication behind Cutter's promises—that he'd be staying, perhaps indefinitely.

Jeremy smiled drowsily and cuddled close to her and fell back asleep.

She lay beside him, thinking of Cutter, knowing that she had to find a way to repay him.

Hours later, Jeremy was still sleeping when Cheyenne arose and went to her room. She sewed Molly Pooh back together, then took a bath and washed her hair with her favorite shampoo that made it smell of honeysuckle and gardenias. She dried the silken masses and pinned them up on top of her head.

The danger was past. Slowly, gently, they would deal with the leftover trauma.

Jeremy was home. That was the main thing. Soon he would be climbing trees. Her garden was cool and opulent and lush once more. The magnolia tree was sprouting new white blossoms by the minute.

Those were signs that it was over. All over.

But it wasn't.

She owed him.

Cutter was in the house somewhere. He was waiting for her. She owed him an apology. More than an apology. She hadn't so much as said thank you.

She hadn't asked him how he had done it.

But the details didn't matter.

Nothing mattered except that Jeremy was safe.

Without Jeremy the mansion had felt like a lifeless tomb. Now, maybe for the first time ever, it felt like home.

She knew that she had to go to Cutter.

Cheyenne felt strange and shy, as scared as a girl. As she knocked on Cutter's bedroom door, she wondered if Cutter would still need her now that he'd found Jeremy.

"Come in."

She fought to contain her thrill at the eagerness she heard in his voice as she opened his door.

For seven years, her anger had shielded and protected her from whatever her true feelings for him were. She remembered how close she had come to making love to him before he had even found Jeremy. Tonight she was even more open, and vulnerable. Therefore, he was more dangerous to her.

She smiled when she saw that he was reading one of *her* books. He shut it quickly and tucked it beneath his pillow so she wouldn't see.

She wore only a green velvet robe tied with a golden cord.

He had shaved and his heavy uncombed black hair glistened from the shower as he lay shirtless in the bed.

He lifted a glossy white magnolia blossom from the bedside table. "That tree of yours...is really something." He took a deep breath as he studied her. "*You're* really something."

His smile lit the room.

Lit her.

"You were reading one of *my* books."

"Because I thought you'd never come. I wanted to read something *predictable*."

"You mean...you wanted something satisfying that has a happy ending."

His eyes were deep and dark and uncustomarily warm as he stared at her. "Yeah. That sounds good."

"I—I didn't mean it to sound so...so Freudian."

Instantly she found herself flushing and staring at his bronzed chest in fascination, wondering if he had anything on under the sheet. She moistened her lips with her tongue, thinking probably he wore no more than she had on under her robe.

She was thinking about Jeremy and how empty and desolate her house and life would have been without him. Cutter had saved her son's life.

I owe him everything. Everything.

He had said he wanted everything.

Maybe if she gave him what he wanted, he would go.

And she would be free again.

What kind of woman was she, to make such an unsavory bargain?

She remembered what had nearly happened between them.

Who was she kidding?

As she stepped inside and shut the door, she felt a tiny pain near her heart at the thought of Cutter ever leaving her. Of his not wanting her in the same deep and eternal way she wanted him. Of his not loving her. Ignoring those long-suppressed feelings, she let her gaze run the length of his body beneath the sheets.

Wrapped in silence, Cutter sat up, watching her as he closed the drawer by the bedside table. Somehow she knew without knowing how that his gun was in that drawer. But she didn't want to think about that or the terrible time of danger they had shared.

It was over.

The danger was past.

The interlaced muscles across his chest and shoulders

and down his arms were strong and hard—taut—as if he, too, found it hard to relax.

"I—I'm sorry for what I said earlier in the library," she managed at last.

"It's okay." His husky voice caressed her, forgave her.

Some new awareness and new awkwardness had come between them. Suddenly there was a new tension in him. As if he were unsure.

"Thank you," she murmured.

"There's no need. Jeremy's my son, too."

Tonight she wanted Cutter to think of her. Only of her.

"Cheyenne, I have a lot of regrets about us."

"You do?"

"All my life I've been so competitive. I had to be first. Maybe I didn't leave room for Martin— Maybe that's why he—"

"Don't."

The last person she wanted to discuss was Martin.

She had to keep this simple. *She owed Cutter.*

She had promised him.

It was dangerous to allow herself to feel more.

"There are no words to thank you," she began.

"I don't want words."

"Do you need anything?" she asked. "A pillow maybe— Or a blanket? I'm sorry I forgot to ask last night. They're in the hall just across— I'll—"

"No. I have everything I need right here."

She turned to go.

"Stay," he whispered. "I picked this flower for your hair. You know what I want."

She froze as he brought the blossom to his nostrils and inhaled. He looked at her. "Come here."

When she hesitated, he said, "Please—"

The single word hung in the darkness. No multitude of words could have been more eloquent than his silence.

Suddenly she was that eager girl again on that windswept island where golden grasses had blown in a winter wind. She was the girl he'd shared his soul with.

His gaze burned her, compelling her nearer. She felt the same fierce need as she had then when he'd lifted the driftwood and she'd willed him to break the glass and make wild, violent love to her.

She remembered how the dune flowers had bloomed. How winter had changed to summer. How she had nearly made love to him just the night before.

A pulse beat in her throat as slowly she undid the golden cord at her waist and pulled it through the loops. Her face was flushed and her eyes flamed as if an inward fire lighted them. She undid her hair and threw back her head, sending spirals of perfumed red curls showering down her shoulders. Her robe fell away, pooling around her bare feet. She dropped the golden cord so that it fell down her thighs, passing between her legs.

In absolute silence his gaze devoured the voluptuous, tawny curves of her body.

For two days and two nights they had lived together under the most terrible tension. During that time his every thought, his every action had been to protect her and their child. He had been infinitely kind to her, infinitely patient. He had made her know that he needed her.

She had promises to keep.

"Come here," he whispered again, his voice rougher now and less sure.

She went to his bed, and the mattress dipped slightly when she sat on its edge.

They were both still and quiet, the only two people in that world of absolute silence. Then he handed her the flower, which she tucked hesitantly into her damp hair.

For a long time they did not speak until finally she lowered her hand to his face. Very gently she touched his lips with the back of a finger. Then with fingertips that had begun to tremble she brushed her hand down the length of his nose.

Just to touch him made her feel the magical bond that had always been there between them.

She sucked in a deep breath and closed her eyes. Like a

blind person, her fingertips fluttered over his every dear feature.

She stroked his rough cheek, his silky hair. How she had missed him. For seven long years she had missed him.

"You found Jeremy. You brought my son home to me."

Cutter sighed. "*Our* son."

"Yes."

"Say it."

"*Our* son."

He smiled. "Was that so hard?"

"Because of you, we're safe."

She felt him tense.

"We did it together," he said.

His skin was smooth and warm, his black hair silken beneath her fingertips. Soon she found that she could not stop touching him.

"Enough," he breathed, tensing again as he caught her wrist. Then he lifted the covers and pulled her beneath them, and she was not in the least surprised to discover that he was naked.

Still, she felt a shock as his long body pressed itself against hers all the way to her toes. Then he wrapped her with his legs and arms and held her close against his powerful, muscular body, in a fiercely intimate embrace while their hunger built.

She had never had another lover, and she had, indeed, been jealous of his. Not that she would ever admit that to him.

"So—you offer yourself like a sacrificial lamb? You believe I'm the worst kind of creep to demand sex in payment for services rendered."

Her long-lashed gaze fell as she clung stubbornly to silence.

"You would not come to me otherwise?" he persisted.

She chewed her lip and looked away.

He grinned as he brushed a hand down her satin-skinned throat and watched her quiver. "So, this isn't good for you?" He trailed his fingers between her breasts, smiling again when she shivered. "So, you haven't missed my touch? Craved it? As much as I have craved yours?"

"You are too conceited for words!"

"I know what I know."

To shut him up, she began to kiss him, but that action merely fueled his argument.

"There. You see," he whispered. "You do want it. Admit it."

Haughtily she withdrew.

When his hands glided over her breasts, she felt consumed by warm, sweet bliss and arched her body against his.

He slid his hand between her legs and deftly stroked her.

"Then why is every flower in your yard and garden in full bloom?"

"I am a talented gardener." She whimpered with pleasure from his touch.

She would never, never admit she had never stopped loving him even though she had wanted to. He was too dark and lethally dangerous. Not the kind of man with whom a smart woman shared her dreams or her soul.

His mouth closed over hers, and a molten flame seared them both. She returned his kisses. Her head moved lower until her lips found his abdomen and that place where a pulse pumped soundlessly.

As her mouth licked against the butterfly movements that betrayed his keen excitement, his callused hands moved in her hair, pushing her head even lower, and he begged, "Kiss me *there*."

A single current of desire pulsed through them both as she licked a path to the intended destination. He groaned aloud as if her slow-flicking tongue against his hot, bare skin consumed him.

He was hard and warm and satin slick.

And when she took him into her mouth, he exploded.

"Oh, God, Cheyenne." He pulled her to him and held her tightly.

Afterward her whole being felt suffused in sunlight, in fluid, radiant color, and in the salty odor and taste of him.

"All those years—when you were married to Martin—I was in hell, Cheyenne."

She put her arms around him, wondering but fearing to ask what he meant. She had thought he hadn't cared, at least not in the way she had. "So was I." She paused guiltily, feeling again that misplaced closeness and that inexplicable bond to him she'd never felt for anyone else. "There's more. I *was* jealous…of those other women…."

He laughed and drew her closer.

"Cutter, I never slept with Martin. Not once. I never wanted to."

Cutter lay on his back with his eyes closed. She could not tell if what she'd said affected him.

Then he said, "God, I thought of you…with him like that…so many times." Dark anguish flickered and made his features grow harsh.

After a long time Cutter moved and dug his fingers into her hair and inhaled her scent. When he exhaled, his warm breath tickled her neck and made her gasp. Then she moved her hands over his body, and he hardened instantly.

"Damn," he whispered as he moved on top of her and then came inside her, making love to her again, almost immediately. And this time everything he did was solely for her pleasure.

The curtains were drawn, and the room was dark. But it was as though he made love to her in a brilliant kaleidoscope of constantly changing colors. One moment he was gentle and worshiping. In the next he was rough and demanding.

His body was lean and tough; he was insatiable and wild. His passion inflamed hers, his appetite made her ravenous. He knew how to keep her at a fever-pitch excitement until she screamed for release.

"Take me, Cutter! Now! I can't wait! Oh, please take me!"

"Only if you'll agree to marry me," he whispered, rolling completely off her.

"Why?"

The emotion in his eyes was deep and dark.

How strange his looking at her that way made her feel. She was all light and jumpy, breathlessly alive, thrillingly happy. But he didn't profess love.

She had used him to get Jeremy back. Was he just using her to hold on to Jeremy?

"Just make love to me," she replied evasively.

"I want more."

She opened her eyes and found that he was still staring at her in that same strangely compelling way. "Marry me, Cheyenne." When she still hesitated: "Damn it. Say yes!"

She felt the force of his powerful will demanding her acquiescence.

When she nodded, he pulled her to him, letting her straddle him this time.

As always they were a perfect fit.

"How can we marry when the past—"

"Maybe if we forget the past for now and concentrate on the future, we'll be okay."

Then he was inside her, filling her with himself, positioning her beneath him after a dozen or so hard strokes. As he drove into her, she arched her body backward and rode a hot wave of endless rapture that took her higher and higher. So high that she felt like a glorious comet spinning out of control, leaving a trail of shimmering ecstasy behind her.

Then it was over, and they were sinking into the warm bed together. He was laughing, holding her close, wrapping her against his heavy body, kissing her again and again.

She lay there in his arms, loving the dampness of his skin and the hardness of his muscled body.

She had thought once would be enough.

But this was better than the island. She wanted more nights with him. Many many more.

Cutter had won.

Whether he loved her or not, she belonged to him now.

Later, when she thought he was asleep, she went to the window and drew back the heavy folds of the drapes with her fingers.

The sun shone with a hard brilliance in the tall trees. It was early yet, a new day; but a day that had lost its morning softness in spite of the flowers that blazed everywhere. The magnolia tree was solid white.

Cutter was not asleep after all. "Come back to bed," he said, his voice tender and yet strangely tense, too. He was holding the squashed magnolia blossom that had fallen from her hair.

He had issued an order, no matter how softly he had spoken.

She dropped the curtain and padded back to the bed where he said, "Later, after we've made love again, I'll go outside and pick another flower for your hair."

And that last time when he took her once more into his arms, she didn't once close her eyes. All her pain and distrust seemed to flow out of her when she climaxed.

He sensed the change in her. Afterward he clung to her, whispering her name and mingling it with husky words of love.

Touched by his tenderness, she lay in the dark wondering if he really meant them.

The night was alive with firelight and fast Spanish guitars, but José Hernando, who prided himself on his strength and his machismo, was not in the mood to celebrate. He felt as weak and violated as a woman he'd once seen after she'd been beaten by a pack of vicious barrio jackals.

Outside his men were drinking and laughing together. José could not join them as was his custom. Not when his mood was so dark.

The barred windows and doors were open in his enormous living room, which served as his big game trophy room, too. Mounted heads of lions, and elephants, and tigers decorated the three-story plaster walls. In one corner stood an entire giraffe. From his heavy leather chair where Hernando sat in sullen drunkenness, he could hear his *mariaches* singing and strumming below in the velvet, flower-scented darkness of the courtyard of his luxurious and seemingly impregnable hacienda.

But no place was impregnable. Not even his home. That bastard Cutter Lord, *el genio,* the international genius, had taught him that.

José could smell wood smoke and beef burning as well as horse dung from the corrals. He could hear his men's laughter grow louder with liquor. He alone could not take part in the festivities.

El genio thought he'd made a fool of him.

It was a warm spring night. There was much rejoicing behind the high adobe walls surrounding Hernando's ranch in northern Mexico. Black-haired women in rebozos stood in doorways surrounded by clusters of dark children. The older boys were each taking a turn with the new bulls in the ring. A valuable wild ocelot that had been caught in a trap had been released as a sacrifice to an ancient god who had been kind.

Gracias a Dios Isabella had been returned unhurt. She'd thrown her arms around her father and with her enormous black eyes focusing on his ruthless face, she had said in her sweetest voice that she didn't want *Papá* to worry, that the men who had taken her had been very nice, that they'd treated her like a princess. They had joked with her and fed her *papas fritas* and *hamburguesas.*

Hernando had stared at her exquisite Spanish face with its patrician nose, classic brow and shapely, rosy lips. She had worn a white mantilla in her hair. She was so innocent. Never had she looked more like her aristocratic mother. Never had he loved her more. He had wanted to die when her mother had died.

Family was everything. Isabella was everything.

Then he had thought of Cutter Lord, the *genius,* who could do no wrong, and never had José hated more, nor lusted for revenge more.

Not even when José had been the poorest and dirtiest boy in the barrio with no real family and the other children had despised him because his plump mother had been a whore had he hated this much. Not even when those gangs of older boys had beaten him with regularity.

Back then he'd had to fight for every scrap of food or starve. Back then he had longed to have a father and a decent mother. To go to school. But the beatings and the poverty had made him tough and hard and determined to rise above that life.

Cutter Lord had been born rich. Everything had come to him the easy way.

Nobody—*nobody*—ever struck out against José and got away with it now that he had power.

"You are a princess, my love," José had whispered, somehow concealing his murderous emotions from her. "I would have died if anything had happened to you."

José was slightly above medium height, with a thick chest and wide shoulders. His features were swarthy. He had a broad, Indian nose, olive dark eyes and the cruel expression of a Spanish conquistador.

"Don't hurt them, *Papá*," she had pleaded, sensing the darkness behind his smile. "They are my friends."

"No, *mi preciosa*, I won't," he had lied in his softest voice even as his rage had threatened to consume him.

A lie was no crime to a man like Hernando. He would be guilty of a far greater crime if he did not avenge his honor. Anger and the fierce desire for vengeance against the man who'd ordered Isabella's kidnapping burned in Hernando's heart. Every time he thought of what could have happened to his precious daughter, he felt the hatred well up within him again, choking him like a fist around his throat, so he could hardly breathe. His men would despise him if he didn't find a way to outsmart the cocky bastard who had made a mockery of him by taking his daughter.

Nobody played José Hernando for a fool.

Nobody.

The ancient juices of vengeance stirred within the black heart of José Hernando.

Cutter Lord had to die.

And so did his family—his woman and her son.

José hadn't killed a human being in a long time.

But this was personal.

He felt his blood race with a wild predatory thrill.

He would do the hits himself.

He would kill the woman and the boy first. He would let Cutter Lord beg for their lives. He would make him crawl.

Then he'd kill him.

Seven

Cheyenne stood at the long windows, staring out at the Gulf, wishing the island wasn't as beautiful as she remembered. She would have preferred any other view to that of dunes cloaked in a green mat of vegetation with dancing pink and yellow wildflowers. Anything would have been better to white beaches and blue surf.

The island stirred painful memories. If Cutter wanted her to forget the past, why had he brought her here?

Cheyenne had another problem with Cutter. In the week that had passed since Jeremy's return, Cutter had grown edgier than ever. And after Jeremy's nightmare three nights ago Cutter had begun prowling their Houston mansion nightly with his gun.

If the danger was past, why was he so uptight? Why had he insisted on leaving Houston and flying them all to his remote island without telling any but his closest associates?

She had wanted to return to Westville to nurse her mother, but he had insisted the island was safer.

Safer?

He had refused to explain what he'd meant by that. For

years Martin had refused to explain himself or the unseen dangers she had sensed. She couldn't face that sort of life again.

She had quarreled with Cutter.

To no avail.

When she had put him on the phone so he could talk to Ivory's nurse, and he had found out that her comatose mother was stable, Cutter had become more adamant that Cheyenne would accomplish nothing by sitting and waiting at her mother's deathbed. Then he had rushed her and Jeremy to his island, saying that marrying her was his number one priority.

"We could get married in Westville—" she'd pleaded.

"We're going to Lord Island. The sooner the better."

Only last night when they'd still been in Houston and she had been making spicy enchiladas from scratch, she had lost her patience and told him that she would never forgive him if he took her to the island instead of to Westville.

"I'll risk it."

Steam and smoke from her bubbling pots had wafted furiously around her.

"No marriage can succeed without trust," she'd said.

"So trust me."

"Or compromises," she'd persisted, stirring a pot so dramatically juice slopped into the flame with a hiss.

"Then you compromise," he had retorted, turning a gas burner lower on the stove top.

"Don't touch a single one of those knobs," she had snapped, batting at his hand with her spatula.

"Your beans were about to burn."

He was right. A fact that infuriated her.

"Do you always have to have your way?" she'd demanded, realizing that she was close to losing control.

"Only when it's important, or I know I'm right."

"Which you think is *all* the time."

He changed the subject. "Do you want me to add water to the beans?"

"Never add water to beans," she snapped. "How can you be so impossibly insensitive? My mother is dying!"

When he laid a hand on her shoulder, she cringed even though his touch was warm and comforting.

His expression darkened. "If it's any consolation, she wouldn't even be aware that you were there."

"How do you know? Anyway, *I'd* know." She drew a deep, trembling breath. "I'll know the rest of my life."

He saw the glimmer of tears in her eyes. "I'm sorry, Cheyenne," he said softly. "But we have to go to the island."

She squeezed her eyes shut and took a deep breath.

Her throat got tight. She was on the verge of tears, and it was all his fault.

She had fought back by sulking.

All through their gourmet Mexican dinner, which she had served in Martin's elegant dining room beneath the Steuben chandeliers. And later she had continued to be moody long into the evening, which they'd spent in the library sorting through Martin's bills.

Cutter had gobbled enchiladas and chalupas, complimenting her cooking, saying she really should write another cookbook, even as he advised her that for normal fare he preferred low-fat meals.

"I will cook whatever I please."

"And *your mother* says I have to have *my* way," Cutter teased, winking at Jeremy as he seized a homemade tortilla and smeared it with chili. "I suppose we'll all get as plump as piglets. I do want to warn you, Cheyenne—I prefer slender women."

When he tried to pass Cheyenne the tortillas, she icily refused the platter.

He raised his eyes and smiled.

She stared at him silently with a dark, glazed expression.

His smiles broadened as he pretended to ignore her scowls and dark silences, but in the end, she'd made him and Jeremy miserable.

Yet, what bothered her the most was that she sensed

Cutter wasn't denying her to be mean, or because he was indifferent. No. There had been kindness and compassion in his eyes.

There was real danger. Uneasily she remembered that when he'd been preparing to pay Jeremy's ransom, he hadn't met with his bankers. No. Cutter had assembled an army. He'd loaded his jet with rifles and high-capacity assault weapons.

What had he done?

She would have to ask him again.

The high grasses in the dunes, which were aflame with wildflowers, swayed in the wind. Cheyenne did feel safer on the island with Cutter than she had in a long time. A million flowers had burst into bloom when their plane had landed. Even so, she could scarcely take her eyes off Jeremy when he played outside. Neither could Cutter who had guards posted everywhere.

From the window near the fireplace she watched Jeremy on the deck as he chucked great handfuls of popcorn into the air. He was laughing and she smiled as greedy gulls whirled and dived, screaming in frenzied excitement all around him.

He had been so afraid at first after he'd come home, but Cutter and she had reassured him. Slowly he regained some of his old confidence. Then just when Jeremy had begun to talk of venturing outside and climbing trees again and calling his friends again, he'd had the nightmare.

He had awakened, screaming that he'd seen and heard Baldy and Kurt in his bedroom. Cutter had taken Jeremy seriously. Within minutes the house had been filled with cops and Cutter's men. By odd coincidence, Kurt had disappeared that same night and all the roses in her garden had withered.

An all points bulletin had been put out on Kurt, but he hadn't been found.

Every night since, Cutter had waited till he thought she was asleep. Then he'd taken his gun and prowled through the house, checking every window, every latch, and every door, especially those near Jeremy's room. Once when she had followed Cutter on his nightly rounds and tripped over a throw rug, he'd whirled and aimed his pistol at her heart.

"Hold it right there!"

She had screamed.

He had jumped and let his gun fall against his jean-clad thigh.

"What the hell do you think you're doing, Cheyenne?" *As if it were her fault.*

But his harsh voice had been as raspy with fear as her breathless scream. When he'd come to her, he'd been shaking almost as much as she.

"Cutter, what are you doing with that...that thing?"

"Just checking around."

"Why?"

"Because—" He looked at her, his eyes bleak and lost. "Just because."

"You shouldn't even have a gun. You could shoot the wrong person. You could have shot me."

He nodded slowly. "You're right. This whole thing has me crazy."

"Why?"

"I can't talk about it."

He reached out and touched her face tenderly as if he wished he could explain, and she knew that her entire arsenal of feminine wisdom against guns stood no chance against his fierce male need to protect and defend.

Blindly she let him take her into his arms, where she buried her face against the hard warmth of his muscular chest. His silence was like a wall between them.

In the safety of his arms, she swallowed a hoarse sob. "Sometimes, even though Jeremy's home and safe, I still feel so scared. Like...now—"

"I know." He stroked her hair.

"Please tell me what's wrong. Not knowing reminds me of how it was with Martin. He never told me..."

"Shhh— I'm not Martin. I'm going to take care of you.

Forever. I swear." He wrapped his arms around her more tightly.

Being held was so wonderful, she stopped asking him questions. Though he didn't confide in her, his silence began to speak to her in a new and magical way. He understood her fear. He shared it. She suddenly felt the depth of his caring, the depth of his need to protect her and their son.

His mouth touched hers, gently at first, and his tongue was warm as it coaxed her lips apart. His rough fingertips began to slide reverently down her cheek. His open palm caressed her breast. Her emotional restraints fell away. So did her fear.

Maybe Cutter didn't love her.

Maybe he never would. Maybe, even though Martin was dead, she would always be a pawn in their war. Maybe he was just using her for sex. Or to get close to Jeremy.

When he had led her back to bed, she had let him make love to her, and the wildness of his need as well as his tenderness, had carried them both to profound new heights.

Fortunately Jeremy had had no more nightmares, and today, as she watched him play outside, he seemed almost normal.

Beyond the smiling boy and his birds, beyond the white beach, a thick lavender sea mist blurred the horizon.

She wished her mother was all right. Maybe then she could enjoy being here with Cutter and her son. But only last night she had dreamed of her mother's marsh drying up and becoming exactly like the arid ranch land that surrounded it. She had dreamed of her mother in her coffin. When Cheyenne had awakened, Cutter had taken her in his arms as she tearfully confessed that she already missed her mother even though she was still alive.

Cheyenne had begged him to let her go home.

"I can't," he had said, holding her and kissing her. "Not yet." He had pressed his mouth to her temple, then her throat. "Darling, I would give you the world if I could."

She had sensed his deep regret and had let him make

love to her. Cheyenne moved away from the window, feeling shame when she remembered how she had screamed with wild joy at the end, how she had needed him, clung to him.

Jeremy had thrown all his popcorn and was now running around, chasing any gulls foolish enough to land. Beyond, the surf roared. The lights of an offshore drilling rig twinkled.

As always the island made her feel cut off from the rest of the world, freer. *Safer.* Which was odd, since she was virtually Cutter's prisoner.

The island and the beach house with its weathered boards and modern, far-flung wings were just as Cheyenne remembered. She wished Cutter had not chosen this spot for their wedding, for it brought back the past, her hopes and dreams, as well as all that had gone wrong between them.

She had been a girl, still young enough, even after Jack's betrayal, to believe in love. She had given herself completely, irrevocably to Cutter only to awaken the next morning and find him gone. His footprints had led to the dock and had not returned, which meant someone, probably by prearranged rendezvous, had come for him by boat. He had taken everything from her and then abandoned her without a backward thought.

Martin had flown in that afternoon. When she had told him about Lyon and that she couldn't marry Martin now, Martin had laughed wildly.

"I know all about it. My bastard of a brother screwed you so I wouldn't marry you."

"What?"

"He told me right before he got on the Lord jet for Singapore. You little fool! Your precious Lyon *is* Cutter. He's done this before. He won't be back."

"But...I saved his life. I— He—"

"I told you how he was. But you're just as dumb as all the others. He has a way of getting around women. He doesn't give a damn about anybody except himself. He's incapable of love."

When she'd discovered she was pregnant, and she tried to call Cutter in Indonesia, his international secretaries would not put her through.

She had tried calling again, only to fail. Someone had erected an impenetrable wall around Cutter, and she was sure that someone had been Cutter.

So—how could she marry him now?

He'd saved Jeremy. He'd promised to protect them with his life.

Cheyenne returned to the fireplace and picked up the large silver-framed photograph of Martin sitting there. In the picture he was smiling as he had never smiled at her or Jeremy after their marriage.

She set the picture on the mantel facedown. Martin had betrayed her. She had thought he felt something for her. But on their wedding night, he had told her that both she and her unborn child disgusted him.

She would not think of Martin nor of the way he had cut her down and belittled her, not today when she was about to marry his brother.

Her wedding gown swirled around her legs and clung to her body. It was a gauzy white cotton dress similar to the one she'd worn the day Cutter had first seen her on the beach.

Cutter had brought it home to her in Houston a few days ago. After she'd opened it, he'd said, "I remember how you looked in that other white dress. I thought I was dying and you were an angel. In a way you were."

Is that what he'd thought?

Then why had he grabbed her ankle and tried to frighten her? Then why had he made love to her and then left her?

So many questions.

Someday she would have to ask them.

She remembered waking up the next morning in bed alone. She remembered searching the island, running desperately toward the beach, following his footprints. When she had seen that they did not return from the dock, she had cut her foot on a broken bottle and had had to hobble a mile back to the beach house.

There she had bandaged her foot and hoped he would return. Only he hadn't. Instead Martin had come and shattered her with his news.

She had fled the island and Martin, running home to her mother. Cheyenne had roamed the marshes as she had when she was a child. She had suffered long days and nights of profound sorrow even before she'd found out she was pregnant. Even though she'd survived, Cutter Lord had made her feel lower and cheaper than anyone in Westville ever had.

And now, today, she was marrying this incredibly cruel man who had hurt her more than anyone ever had. This cold man who put his own needs before hers, this man who had refused to let her go home when her mother was so ill.

And yet—

He could be so tender. She understood him and felt bonded to him in deep, undefinable ways. Would he ever feel the same?

Since Jeremy's return, Cutter and she had avoided any discussion of the past. Instead they had concentrated on making Jeremy feel safe and wanted and on straightening out Martin's messy financial affairs.

When she had been most furious at Cutter over her mother, she had been stunned when a huge truck had arrived with all of her things that had been sold at the auction. Cutter had confessed to buying them all, but he had not even let her finish thanking him, saying that as her future husband, it was his duty and his pleasure to provide for her.

His generosity and his tenderness and his protectiveness puzzled her. Did he merely want his son? And the pleasure of her body? Or did he, too, really want more?

Cutter, his dark face filled with uncustomary warmth, strode across the deck toward her. She thought of all the old hurts and of his more recent tyranny and forced her heart to freeze. Then she saw Jeremy who'd grown bored

with the gulls, trailing behind his father as if he were a
happy puppy. How alike they were, she thought, almost
resenting their newfound easiness with each other. Both
were tall and tanned. Both knew exactly what they wanted
and were determined to have it. Both knew how to make
her dance to their tune.

One thing was indisputable: Jeremy, who had been
starved for a father's affection, already adored Cutter. The
boy had instantly taken Cutter's part in the matter about
his grandmother, saying, "Granny knew we loved her. She
wouldn't know if we were there or not."

For Jeremy's sake, Cheyenne tried to smile and left the
fireplace and threw open the patio door so they could enter.

Cutter was wearing jeans and a white shirt. As was Jeremy who copied his father in everything. "Everybody's
ready for the ceremony, honey," Cutter said mildly.

"Yeah, Mom. Uncle Cutter says we can't cut the wedding cake till you two get married. And I'm real hungry."

"Give me a minute or two alone," she whispered, smiling.

When she glanced at Cutter, her smile faltered. What was
happening to her? Part of her resented his new power over
her life. Part of her longed for it. And every night she
welcomed his touch.

With a blush she fought not to think of all the times
they'd made love since that first night after he'd brought
Jeremy to her. Of how her passion seemed to grow fiercer
every night. Of how even during the day she felt fluttery
with unwanted excitement whenever he was near.

Cutter leaned down and kissed her lightly on the cheek.
When she jumped back, he slid his arm around her waist.
"Please, Cutter," she whispered, pushing him away. "Not
now...when everybody is looking."

"Right," he murmured in a hard voice. "We're getting
married in about five minutes, and you don't want me
touching you. Come outside, Jeremy."

"Uncle Cutter gave me the rings to hold, Mom." Jeremy
patted his pocket importantly.

"Cutter, I—I—"

"I got the message," he rasped.

No, you didn't.

Suddenly her mouth felt too dry to speak. She felt stricken as he walked away.

Alone once more, her emotions tore at her. She paced the huge, charming room with views of the Gulf.

What kind of person am I?

I don't want to marry this man. I hardly ever know what he's thinking or why he does what he does. Yet...I do want to be with him. No! I can't want to marry him. And it's wrong of me to marry a second time for the wrong reasons.

And yet...

She rushed outside, her mind in a frenzy. When she started to cry, Cutter gently brushed her tears away. She resented the way his light touch tapped into her heart and soul and psyche.

"Don't think about what it all means now," he whispered. "We'll sort it out later."

He handed her a bouquet of wildflowers and led her to the altar that he and Jeremy had constructed together out of driftwood.

The wedding was small and simple. No family other than Jeremy attended. Her mother was far too ill, and Cutter hadn't invited his family. His vice president, O'Connor, whom she'd hit with her giant pansies, was there as a witness.

As the preacher ran through the ceremony, Cheyenne gripped Cutter's arm and fought to ignore the icy cramps knotting her stomach. In spite of the swaying grasses and frothing surf, the wedding seemed cold and mechanical. Her mother was very ill. Her father long dead. Her sister had always hated her. Cheyenne thought of the future and the long years ahead when she would have no one to turn to but Cutter. She had hoped for a real marriage. For closeness and trust.

For true love.

What did Cutter really want?

At the end of the service, Cutter took her into his arms and tipped her chin back. When she looked up into his dark eyes, a blazing rush spiraled through her. Then he smiled and kissed her. His mouth was warm and familiar, and yet she felt that some invisible barrier was there between them. She knew him as a lover and yet in some ways he was still a stranger.

Would her husband always keep more secrets from her than he shared? Suddenly he became grave, as if the prospect of their future worried him, too. When he squeezed her hand reassuringly, her wedding ring cut into her fingers and made her flinch.

After the short ceremony, Jeremy hugged them, his eyes alight. "Now I have a mother *and a father.*"

"Yes," Cutter said, putting his arm around his bride's slender waist. "And I have a wife and a son."

A lump swelled in Cheyenne's throat.

Cutter put his other arm around Jeremy. "We're going to be a real family."

Were they? Did Cutter really believe that?

The moment passed, and her foolish hope died as Cutter grew moodier. Not that he seemed as filled with doubt as she. He insisted on cutting the wedding cake, which she had made, and sharing a piece with her, teasing her that everybody said her food had aphrodisiac qualities....

It was late when Jeremy, who had stuffed himself on wedding cake—which had given him a sugar high—finally wound down enough to go to bed.

Minutes later Cutter carried Cheyenne over the threshold into their bedroom.

"At last," he said, bolting the door. The eagerness in his voice and in his hands sent an odd shiver through her.

He ripped his shirt off. "I thought this day would never end."

"Was it so awful for you then?" she whispered, not ready to admit to her own quickening desire.

His eyes were hot. So hot, she blushed.

"Awful? Why do you say that?"

"I don't know what you're thinking or feeling."

"Think this—I was in a fever to have you, to marry you," he said, going to her and pulling her roughly to him. "Feel this." He shoved her against the door. He was all taut muscle molded over strong bones. Slowly he bent her head back across his arm and ran his tongue along her collarbone. Then he kissed her mouth. Soon his lips moved across her face and throat with such feverish intensity that she clung to him. He licked her nipples until all she could see or feel was a haze of erotic colors and sensations. His skin was sandpaper-rough and yet satin-smooth. His mouth was hot, but his hands were cool. Somehow her own shaky fingertips found themselves in his hair. She could feel his body pressing more tightly against her. He shifted his weight, slipping his hands beneath her to cup her bottom, lifting her higher so that she could feel his hard male arousal.

In the next instant she was drowning in pleasure.

Through the long years of her first marriage there had been many many nights when she had lain awake in her bed alone and dreamed of Cutter making love to her in this room again.

Had he really ever dreamed of her? Longed for her as she had longed for him? Just once?

Only once had he said anything to indicate that he had.

"Cheyenne. Oh, Lord. Cheyenne—"

He swung her off her feet and carried her to the bed where he finished undressing her with hands that were swift and sure and warm against her icy skin. His fingers slipped buttons through thickly threaded loops. Then he caressed her bare flesh beneath the gauzy white fabric.

She undressed him, too, swiftly, eagerly, kissing the hard contours of his chest where his heart pounded so violently.

Soon their clothes, his jeans and shirt, her cotton dress, lay together in a tangled heap.

He got into bed and lay down on top of her.

They were married.

She was his wife.

The thought of it made her sigh with inexplicable longing for a true marriage.

He gazed down at her, his harsh face tender in the dying
light.

She tried to tell herself that what they did at night was
only about sex.

But the sweetness in his eyes warred with the violence
of his need. When his hard mouth closed on hers with in-
finite gentleness, she felt cherished.

Not that he said he felt that way with words.

His mouth clung to hers a long while—gently still and
then more fiercely. When she was breathless from his
kisses, he trailed his mouth downward, between her breasts,
over her belly, between her thighs.

With a tremor, she parted her legs.

He was her husband now.

She told herself that he was dangerous to her, that his
being her husband meant nothing. Nothing. That theirs was
merely a marriage of convenience.

But the tenderness beneath Cutter's passion moved her
to feel new tenderness for him. Tears of joy came into her
eyes as Cutter's hands and lips and tongue devoured her
and she found rapture and soul-deep meaning in his lovemaking.

Afterward, when he had brought her to ecstasy and found
his own, he lay down beside her as if he were a heavy,
sated animal, his arm thrust across her waist to hold her
near.

And as they lay in the dark, their warm, sweaty bodies
touching, the need to have each other again shook them
with unexpected force.

"I want to go down to the beach and make love in the
surf," she breathed into his ear.

He brushed damp tendrils from her brow. "Where I first
saw you, where you saved me," he said softly, surprising
her for he spoke as if that were a cherished memory.

"Why did you marry me?" she asked.

"I wanted you," he replied. "I couldn't stop myself. Do you understand? I had to have you. Even if you really are some sort of magical witch who can destroy me."

His words crushed her.

The water, which was washed with moonlight, was cold when they raced hand in hand into the surf. He sank to his knees in the splashing water and then lay looking up at her for a moment before pulling her down in the silvery froth on top of him. Soon they were so hot and eager, the coldness of the water didn't matter.

A wave crashed over them.

Then another, splashing them with liquid icy diamonds. More waves.

But their bodies, which were locked together, rose and fell in the dark swirls of shimmering wetness.

Afterward he dried her with a warm towel.

Laughing, they ran back to the house.

They showered together. Slept together.

And awoke together.

But it was different in the morning.

Her wedding bouquet had completely withered. As had all the flowers on the island.

The incredible closeness she had felt for him when the island lay bathed in warm moonlight dissolved in the first cold rays of the dawn. Guiltily she remembered her mother and his refusals and was warier of a man who could make love to her with such passion and refuse such a request.

As he was wary of her.

Nor could she forget that he had abandoned her when she'd been pregnant.

He, too, had his own demons and was grim-faced over matters that he did not confide. With little more than a brief kiss and an uncertain glance toward the other, they arose and got dressed.

Thus, it seemed that their life together was divided into two worlds. Their nights held fierce, erotic pleasure and incredible closeness; their days awkward estrangement and moody silences. And every morning a door seemed to seal between these two worlds.

During their week-long honeymoon Cheyenne noticed the many morning glories and evening primroses on the island. Such flowers reminded Cheyenne of her marriage since they opened their blooms by night and reached full beauty at dawn. But once their fragile petals were touched by the morning sun, they began to wither.

Every night Cheyenne would gather armfuls of morning glories and evening primroses. She would place them in a vase by her window. Every morning she would awaken to find the glorious yellow flowers with their thin-petaled blossoms as dead as her husband's night passion.

Still, every evening she would race to the dunes right before dusk and pick armfuls of these flowers and then run back to the house where Cutter was waiting eagerly for her.

On the final afternoon of their honeymoon, O'Connor arrived by private plane, bringing the usual mail along with a wedding present that had been hand-delivered to her mansion in Houston. Cheyenne wondered who could have sent a present since none of her friends knew of her marriage.

The lavishly wrapped box with her name on it was tied with a wide, white satin ribbon.

Jeremy ran up just as Cheyenne set it on a table and tore away the glossy paper. Jeremy snatched off the lid, and lifted out a card taped to the top of the tissue paper.

Just as she read the bold black scrawl, Cutter burst into the room, his arms full of wild dune flowers that instantly began to wither.

"What's that?" he demanded.

"Cutter, do you know anybody named José?"

She was too busy tearing into the tissue to notice that Cutter's shocked silence expanded to fill one second, then two.

Dying flowers exploded out of Cutter's arms as he lunged toward her.

"Darling, don't—"

He was too late.

She had already seen the three horrifying photographs.

When she gasped, Jeremy grabbed the pictures and stared, his young dark face draining of color.

As if drawn by a hypnotic force, Cheyenne stared at the pictures again.

Then her thin screams pierced the silence.

Next she staggered backward, her hands clutching her throat, as she gulped deep shuddering breaths and fought nausea.

She couldn't stop gasping and panting. It was as if someone were holding a hand over her face and she could get no oxygen. Her arms began to tingle. Her hands went numb.

Bile bubbled up her throat.

After she threw up, she burst into tears.

Her feet and legs were going numb now.

Cutter grabbed her. "Take deep, regular breaths!"

But she was too hysterical to listen to him.

"You knew," she whispered. "You knew. All the time you knew."

"No."

His concerned face blurred dizzily and then was lost in darkness.

She couldn't feel any part of her body now.

As she stumbled forward, collapsing into Cutter's strong waiting arms, she thought she was dying.

But she only fainted.

Eight

There was a faint sound at the bedroom door as Cutter flipped a magazine page noiselessly.

Cheyenne sat up in bed, as alert as a cat, her heart beating nervously as if she sensed danger, yet, without knowing what had awakened her.

The bedroom was quiet. Normal. The sun was shining through the dazzlingly clean windowpanes of Cutter's beach house.

Outside a dozen gulls soared and dived, making lazy circles against a hazy blue sky. Beyond the dunes the Gulf was serene; the surf no more than a gleaming curl licking buff-colored sand.

Cutter was sprawled in the overstuffed blue chair next to her bed. His long lean body looked very relaxed in his faded jeans, blue cowboy shirt, boots and huge silver belt buckle. He was reading a business magazine, as if he were a normal, concerned Texas husband whose wife was ill with a simple stomach virus, as if theirs was a normal, loving marriage.

For a minute or two, the inviting beauty of the scene and

the comfort of his presence made her feel completely disoriented. Then she saw his black pistol on the table between them, and the horrible memory of the pictures of Kurt's dead body came back to her.

Suddenly she felt like a stranger in her own life.

"Kurt's eyes were bulging open," she whispered in a ragged, torn voice as if he hadn't seen the photographs, too.

"Honey, Kurt was one of them."

"His awful eyes were just staring, not seeing—" Her voice was low and hoarse. It hurt her throat to speak.

"Don't think about it," Cutter said simply, calmly, snapping his magazine shut and tossing it on the table beside his gun. "All that matters is that you're feeling better."

Who was this man she had married? That he could be so coldly unmoved by such a monstrosity? As if it were an ordinary event to him.

Martin had told her often enough that Cutter was considered lethal and cold when it came to business, that he had added to his family's immense fortune and made money all over the world. That he had worked in the darkest parts of Africa and South America as well as war-torn lands in the Orient. That no one who operated on his international scale was tougher.

What had Cutter had to do to succeed on such mega-levels? Had he killed? Would he?

Virile and male, his ambition and determination were etched in his harsh features for anyone to see. The arrogant thrust of his jaw and chin accented the cynical lines carved on either side of his hard, insolent mouth. His shoulders were broader than the big blue plush chair he sat in, so that in her present mood he seemed both terrifyingly powerful and dangerously ruthless.

She had never known anyone like him. He'd gotten a trifle edgy this past week, but he hadn't acted shaken or shown fear the way she would have. The way Martin had. There was a dark, forceful side to Cutter, an icy control at his core that terrified her.

All week he had expected something like this. But he'd

kept silent and hidden his emotions and thoughts behind a stonelike mask.

Now she knew why he hadn't let her out of his sight. Why he had brought her to a remote island instead of Westville.

She tilted her chin defiantly. "Where's Jeremy? How is he?" she asked, her tone rebellious.

"Fine."

How could he sound so cool?

"Fine? What does that mean? Is he upset? Of course, he's upset— I mean—"

"He's one tough kid. Sure, he's worried. We talked about it. He understands the situation. He trusts me to get us out of it."

"What's he doing right now? This very minute?"

"He's in his room playing with his computer. He's concerned about you."

"I don't want him out of this house! Do you understand? Those monsters took him once. They could—" She burst into tears and then fought against her rising panic.

Cutter nodded grimly. "Look, I doubt José is going to launch some full-scale assault on my island. He's made his point. He'll wait till we relax. Until we're easier targets."

Targets?

Cutter's icy calm was unbelievable.

"So—are you going to tell me who José is?"

"You and Martin owed José Hernando five million dollars. Like most reasonable businessmen, José likes to be paid."

Most reasonable... "So, José took Jeremy?"

There was a faint sound at the door, but neither she nor Cutter paid any attention to it.

"Not José personally. But he ordered it."

"But if you paid him the ransom, we should be safe—"

"Yeah. Maybe...we would be *if*—" Cutter's quiet tone wasn't reassuring.

"Maybe? If? What am I hearing?" Trembling, she sat up higher in bed.

He leaned closer, drawing her gaze to his. For a second, the longest second of her life, Cheyenne held her breath. Then he spoke. "But that's not how it is. We're in more danger than ever, Cheyenne."

"Why?" Her soft voice sounded strangely fierce. She was remembering the assault weapons, the tough-looking army, all the rounds of ammunition. Everything he hadn't trusted her enough to explain. Everything she hadn't dared to ask about.

"I didn't pay the ransom." His tone was low and deep, as before, and yet different. The light in his eyes had died; they were cold and utterly blank. "That's why José sent us those pictures. To warn us."

"That we're next?"

Cutter nodded.

Some part of her had known all along.

Her voice softened ominously. "This is all your fault. If you'd just done what he said—"

"Hey, sorry—" All goodwill vanished from his voice. "I play by my own rules. Not some gangster's. José took my son. So, I took his daughter."

Cheyenne's heart began to beat very fast. "You what?"

"I let her go when we got Jeremy."

"Why couldn't you just pay him?"

"Because, my naive innocent, he would have killed Jeremy for sure."

"You couldn't possibly know that."

"Yeah, well, you can have those illusions because you haven't had to live like I have. I've dealt with bastards like him before. Too many times. I paid a ransom. Once. Do you want to know what happened? First, I lost my money. As if I gave a damn for the pittance those starving wretches demanded. But I did give a damn when they threw the decomposed body of my young executive onto my front lawn with a bullet between his eyes. Jorge wasn't much more than a boy, but he'd seen his kidnappers' faces. They were afraid he'd put them behind bars." Beneath Cutter's cool voice and stony expression, she felt the violence in him beating its way to the surface. "They didn't get off so easy. Jorge had been like a brother to me. The kind of brother I never had. I handpicked some professionals. We hunted his killers down—one by one— It took me six months to track their leader."

"What happened then?"

Cutter's face darkened. His black eyes glittered. "I never lost another man in that country."

Sensing the terrible deep pain beneath his hardness, she felt a strange pull from him, a crazy wish to forget her own anger and comfort him.

"Why didn't you tell me the truth?" she persisted obstinately.

"Because I knew you'd panic. Just like you're doing now."

She sat up higher. "Don't speak to me like I'm a first-grader. Of course, I'm panicking. A stranger sends me pictures of my bodyguard's corpse—"

Her prim reprimands infuriated him. "Some bodyguard. You're lucky Kurt didn't slit your throat while you slept. We're lucky José took him out."

Lucky— "You deliberately put us in danger."

Cutter's lips thinned. "Hey, you and Martin borrowed the money, sweetheart. From a very dangerous man. You didn't pay it back. I'm just picking up the pieces."

"Well, you're doing a lousy job."

"Jeremy is still alive. So are you. Where would you be if I hadn't come the night you called?"

"What does that matter, if we have to hide out? If José is going to kill us anyway?"

"Damn it, Cheyenne!" Cutter exploded out of his chair, knocking over the flimsy bedside table. His pistol, the brass-shaded lamp and his magazine crashed onto the floor. "Can't you, just once, show a little faith in me?"

Before she could cringe away from him, he sank down on the bed beside her. His long fingers clamped around her wrists, drawing her closer. The inarticulate sound he made under his breath was pure rage. "I want to get something real straight, honey. Jeremy's kidnapping, Kurt's death—this whole business—isn't my fault!''

In the thundering aftermath of his absolute silence, she felt his fingers bruising the soft skin at the sides of her wrists as his grip tightened.

''You're hurting me,'' she whispered.

Without a word, he yanked his hands free of her as if in disgust and straightened wearily.

Slowly he leaned down and picked up his gun. His lean, muscular body was rigid with tension as he reined in his emotions. Ignoring her, he handled his revolver expertly, checking it, spinning the cylinder, dusting off the broken light-bulb fragments. When he set it down again, she saw that his hand was shaking, as hers was. Then his muscles tightened, and he regained control.

Even before he spoke in that quiet and yet menacing tone, she realized he was still furious. ''Maybe you and Martin were right for each other after all. The one thing I could always count on from my family, especially Martin, was that they would always think the worst of me. I grew up with that. Martin was the extroverted son my parents longed for and loved—their golden, fun-loving boy—so, I turned to books and math and business where I excelled. I worked very, very hard to prove myself to them. I learned to be outgoing. But my parents didn't care. They just wanted me to help Martin, to take care of Martin. Martin resented my talents. None of them ever realized or cared about what I wanted. They said I was like my money-grabbing grandfather who put us all on easy street but was vulgar and hard and treated us harshly. My first wife was just like them. It didn't take me long to figure out all she thought I was good for was to make money. I decided maybe she was right. I paid her off and got rid of her. I gave up on love after that and paid attention to business. Until I met you.''

His tormented gaze never left her face.

''Cutter—''

''Damn it. I tried to forget you, but you ate at me all

those years you were married to Martin. I used to see families in cars or restaurants. There'd be a man and a woman and a little girl and boy. Children. A family. I hungered for a family like that. I would think of you and Martin— God, I envied him so much. I don't know what kept me sane.'' He paused. ''When Martin died and I learned José was after you, I thought I couldn't bear losing you again. Not if there was even the slightest chance that we could be—'' His voice broke. ''But, I swear, if it wasn't for Jeremy, I'd walk out of this room right now and never come back!''

He'd given up on love. Until her.

He'd thought he couldn't bear losing her—

He'd wanted a family. A normal family.

Her heart hammered; her throat went dry.

His speech had jolted her. Still, she resisted believing in him. How could she let her foolish emotions overrule her intellect?

He stared at her, his breathing ragged. Tension, thick and hot and silent, hung like a pall between them. ''You think I'm some kind of monster like José.'' His voice was chillingly silken.

''No— I—I—''

Before she could adequately deny his accusation, their bedroom door swung open. Jeremy, who'd obviously been eavesdropping, burst inside and ran to her. ''Mom, I'm glad Da— I mean Uncle Cutter saved me. He's going to shoot Baldy and that José guy, and we'll all be okay. You'll see.''

''That's right, *son*,'' Cutter said coldly.

Jeremy beamed.

''You two have obviously discussed this,'' she whispered. Tensely she turned to Cutter. ''So, how are you going to work this miracle? I want specifics. What exactly are you going to do?''

Cutter's icy gaze froze her. ''Whatever I have to.''

Whatever unspeakable horror that meant.

''Dear God—'' She turned away.

''Don't be so mean, Mom! Uncle Cutter's not the bad guy!''

Jeremy leapt from the bed and moved closer to Cutter. He took his father's hand and held on to it.

She was amazed that Jeremy, who had been kidnapped by these monsters, could be taking this so calmly. Clearly Cutter had brainwashed him.

Never had father and son looked more alike than they did in that moment as their perceptive black eyes warily studied her as if her being female made her an alien species. Their grim smiles vanished at precisely the same moment. They looked away from her and nodded at each other, at precisely the same moment as if there was a soul-to-soul, utterly male, genetic understanding between them.

For an instant she felt ganged up upon. It was as if they were on one wavelength and she another.

"Dear God." She buried her face in her hands. "What's happening? I—I should never, never have married you! I don't want Jeremy to grow up and be hard and cold like you!"

"Hey— I stuck my neck into the noose for you," Cutter said. "Show a little gratitude."

"Gratitude?"

"Yeah, Mom. He means quit being so mean to him."

"Mean? Oh—" She buried her face in her pillow.

The last thing she heard before the door closed behind them was Jeremy's piping voice.

"Don't worry, Uncle Cutter. She never sulks very long."

"I'm not sulking!" she screamed. "It's perfectly normal to be upset—"

She wadded up her pillow and threw it at the closed door.

Jeremy's defection to Cutter was unendurable.

All his life Jeremy had longed for a father. Martin had belittled him for being so quiet and smart. The few crumbs of affection Martin had tossed Jeremy had been done mainly to spite her.

Now, for the first time Jeremy shared an instinctive closeness to a man he admired—his biological father. Cutter had been unfailingly kind and attentive.

Every night he went into his son's room where they read

and talked, where Jeremy asked him endless questions. All
of which Cutter, who had told her he'd been a tiresomely
curious child, patiently tried to answer. Cutter had told her
that his childhood had been lonely and unhappy, that Martin had been the favorite, and that he had escaped first into
books, then his studies, and later his businesses.

*Father and son loved each other. They understood each
other.*

*Cutter loved Jeremy and wanted to make him part of his
life.*

Just as she did.

As a child she had longed for her own father. Every time
she had competed against and bested Chantal, it had been
to win her father's love and respect. Whenever Ben had
shown up at a school function, she had dreamed of him
praising her and inviting her home to his big ranch house
where he had lived. She had imagined him making Chantal
accept her. Only Ben West had never claimed her; he'd
witnessed all her pitiful attempts to win his love as well as
her shame. He'd hung his head. But he'd let it continue.

On the other hand, Cutter had come to her when she and
Jeremy were in danger. He had risked his life for them.

She thought about what Cutter had said about dreaming
of a family. Of having a little girl and a boy.

*In spite of the past and all that had gone wrong and was
still wrong between them, Cutter and she were becoming a
family.*

As this knowledge began to glow inside her like a warm
fire near her heart, her stubborn, irrational anger toward
Cutter began to lessen.

Not that she was anywhere near being ready to open her
door and tell him she was sorry.

Nine

The silence from *her* end of the hall was deafening.

Cutter had spent his life dealing with petty, third-world tyrants. Maybe Cheyenne was sweet. Maybe she was pretty. But she could hold her own with the most difficult despot when it came to being stubborn.

For five hours she had kept her door closed.

For five hours the atmosphere had felt heavy and brooding and made Cutter edgier and edgier.

While Cheyenne kept to her room, Cutter and Jeremy camped in Jeremy's room. Cutter worked on the computer while Jeremy read with his usual thirst for knowledge.

But they left their door open.

The better to see her, and hear her, should she open hers.

Computer printouts, half-opened encyclopedias, and local history books were now strewn all over Jeremy's floor. In spite of his concern about Cheyenne, Cutter had been starved for Jeremy's company so long, he enjoyed spending any time, even these tense hours with the boy. It pleased him enormously that Jeremy was so intellectually precocious.

Jeremy looked up from the history book he'd been quietly absorbed in. "Uncle Cutter, did you know that in 1834 the remains of a pirate's camp were found on this island? It says right here that large iron rings were implanted deep in the sand. Some people thought the rings were used to moor small boats rowed in from bigger ships." When Cutter didn't answer fast enough, Jeremy said, "I guess they rusted out a long time ago, huh?"

"I've never seen them."

"Maybe we could look for 'em sometime— Together..." Jeremy's voice trailed away.

"Sure."

They smiled at each other and then pretended to go back to their individual pursuits.

Suddenly Jeremy's glossy black head peeped up over his book again.

"Hey, did you know that a lady on Mustang Island in the 1880s found a chest filled all the way to the top with silver coins?"

"No," Cutter replied.

"I wish I could find something like that. Did you ever look for treasure?"

Cutter began to tap on the keyboard. "All the time."

"Where?"

"Everywhere."

"Oh, I get it. You're talking about making money."

Cutter stopped typing and turned to Jeremy. "How come you read so much?"

"'Cause I like to. Mom taught me to read when I was three. With a phonics tape. I got passed out of first grade after a month 'cause I already knew everything and was getting bored and being bad."

"I used to read so much my mother had to make me go outside and play with other kids."

"Same here," Jeremy said. The odd intent look he suddenly shot his father caught at Cutter's heartstrings.

Silence.

"That's not why I really read," Jeremy blurted. "I read

'cause Mom and Dad fought all the time and I didn't want to think about it.''

"They fought, huh?"

"Mostly my dad just screamed at my mother and she got real quiet."

Cutter's mouth thinned.

Jeremy's black eyes grew as huge as wafers. Then out of the blue came the question.

"You're my real dad aren't you?"

The sudden silence grew electric.

Cutter had dreaded this moment. Now that it was here, he wasn't ready. Hell, he'd never be ready.

He drew a long, shallow breath. "How long have you known?"

"A while." Flushing, Jeremy looked down at his book again. He began fiddling with a page corner, flipping it till it tore. "I heard Dad—I mean Martin—say something really mean to Mom once about me and her and you."

The bedroom grew very quiet again.

Cutter didn't know what to say.

"I felt real bad," Jeremy continued shyly. "Dad was really mad. I didn't think he liked me. Or Mom. He called her a bad name and she cried. I was all mixed up. I—I didn't want to be your son, either."

Cutter nodded bleakly. "If only I'd have known—" He broke off. He couldn't have done a damned thing if he'd known.

Suddenly it seemed to him that he and Jeremy were strangers, that layers of pain and misunderstanding stood between them, that they had missed too much and hurt each other too much to ever get past it. Cheyenne had said she didn't want Jeremy to grow up and be like him.

Jeremy looked down at his book again.

Wanting to erase the past seven years and start over, Cutter turned silently back to his blank computer screen and fought to pretend nothing had been said.

But some things can't be unsaid or so easily forgotten.

The yellow cursor blinked madly, taunting him.

Cutter switched off the computer. In the same fraction of a second that he spun his chair around, Jeremy looked up from his book, his eyes huge.

Hell, they were probably no bigger than his own.

"I'm glad you married Mom," Jeremy said quietly.

Cutter nodded, mute, all his own fierce emotions on that subject blocked.

But when Jeremy got up, he rose stiffly, too.

As they stood there, looking at each other, Cutter suddenly felt too heavy-limbed to take a single step.

Jeremy's black gaze widened. "Dad— I—I—" In the next instant he was flying across the room into his father's arms. "I love you, Dad. I love you," he said thickly, through tears.

"Jeremy." Cutter wrapped his arms around the boy, squeezing him tightly. He realized with a pang that he should have found a way to reach out to his son long before now. He should have claimed him and protected him from Martin.

Jeremy needed him.

Suddenly Cutter felt unleashed. Torrents of blocked feelings flowed from him. Seven years of withheld paternal emotion. Seven years of anguish and loneliness.

"I love you, too, Jeremy."

He repeated the words softly, and then kept repeating them, unable to stop saying them.

"What about Mom?" Jeremy asked a long time later.

Silence followed.

"I'm glad I married your mom, too," Cutter admitted grimly, hugging the boy closer and ruffling his hair. "I just hope she won't stay mad forever."

"She won't."

"How do you know?"

A shy, radiant smile broke across Jeremy's face. "Because I've got a plan."

"It better be good."

Jeremy's smile was a devilish grin now. "Do you re-

member how she came running the night of my nightmare—''

"Don't even think about it!"

The hours dragged by.

Cutter lay alone in the dark, watching the intermittent
bursts of lightning and listening to the roar of the wind and
rain and the blasts of thunder. The couch was too short and
the cushions too big and soft. He kept twisting and turning.
Every time he drifted off, erotic fantasies about Cheyenne
woke him up again.

He kept dreaming of her naked. Of her deliciously warm
body next to his. And he ached to be inside her.

Then his body would stiffen; he'd break out in a cold
sweat. And wake up. It had happened dozens of times. It
was frustrating as hell.

He gripped the edge of the couch. Why was he torturing
himself?

She was mad at him.

He was mad at her.

She didn't love him. They had too many problems to
ever work them out.

He threw off his sheet and sat up, feeling hot and
wretched.

How many hellish nights had he lain awake like this and
imagined her across some ocean in the arms of his brother?

His lips twisted into a bitter smile.

Too damned many.

And now tonight, even though he was her husband, she
had put him into the same hellish fix.

What had he done to deserve such punishment?

Still, there was one unforgettable truth.

She had slept with him.

Only him.

In all the years of her marriage to Martin, never once
had she slept with his brother.

Maybe Cheyenne didn't love him. Maybe Cutter didn't

love her. Maybe he couldn't ever, after what she'd done and said.

But damn it, her fidelity meant a lot.

He drew a shaky hand across his face.

He thought about it at the oddest times.

And he wondered why the hell it meant so much to him.

Cheyenne flung her sheets aside and rose from her bed and began to pace. Rain lashed the windows, sending monstrously huge, sparkling drops rushing down the glass. Wind beat against the shutters.

She stared outside, terrified.

The grasses whipped in the storm. Sand was blowing across the deck into the pool.

Storms could be a bad sign.

She kept seeing Kurt's dead body in the photograph. She kept imagining his murderer arriving by boat, as Cutter had so long ago.

If only she could stop thinking about it. Stop feeling the awful fear. Stop wanting to run down the hall to Cutter.

A tear trickled down her cheek.

Then another.

She tried to brush them away, but that only made them rush downward in a hot cascade.

It was all so awful. Everything Martin had done. Jeremy's kidnapping. Kurt—

Why had she and Martin lived so high? Why had she let Martin borrow the money? Why had it been so important to them both to be somebody?

Now she wanted simpler things. Love. A family.

Most of all she wanted Cutter. She didn't care what he had done in the past.

Maybe he'd coldly abandoned her. Maybe she had felt forced to marry Martin, but Cutter had come to her when she was lonely and in terrible danger. He had saved Jeremy. He had been gentle and tender—in his way. He was her husband. Her lover.

Her only lover.

She felt so empty and lost without him. She wanted to be wrapped in his hard, strong arms.

To feel safe again.

To feel loved and wanted.

But could a man who had lived as he had love her or trust her? Was he capable of just using her for sex just so he could have Jeremy?

She couldn't fathom the kind of life that had made Cutter so tough and hard and fearless.

Was he as incapable of love as Martin had always said? Or had Martin been blinded by jealousy and painted the wrong picture? Had Cutter been the lonely son, the left-out son?

One thing she knew. Cutter was brave and strong and willing to sacrifice himself for her and his son.

The past was the past.

In that moment, she suddenly knew that she wanted Cutter too much not to try to give him the benefit of the doubt.

Jeremy was awakened by a sudden, abrupt buzzing of his alarm clock from under his pillow. It took him a minute to remember why he'd set his alarm. Still, he was so drowsy he would have ignored it except the clock rumbled and made the pillowcase tickle his ear.

Sleepily, clumsily, he jabbed at the buttons of his tiny portable alarm till it went off.

He needed to pee, so he got up and went to the toilet. After that he got back into bed and forced himself to sit there and concentrate on his plan. Groggily he focused on the terrifying feelings he'd had when Baldy had come into his Houston bedroom and pounced on him when he'd been asleep.

He didn't like remembering his high-pitched screams. They had rolled out of his body like waves as he'd been dragged out of his room.

He forced himself to remember Molly Pooh's head flying off. The roof of his mouth went dry as he relived the fear he'd felt when Baldy had shoved him down the stairs.

Nobody had come to help him that night when he'd screamed.

Not Kurt.

Not Mrs. Perkins.

Not his mom or his dad.

He got scared all over again just thinking how alone and little and small he'd felt.

But they'd come to him when he'd had his nightmare.

They'd do the same tonight.

Jeremy opened his mouth, and let out a massive, ear-splitting yell.

When he screamed a second time, he heard *her* door open.

Then *his*.

Yes! Yes! Jeremy slugged his pillow in triumph.

Inspired, he screamed again and again, three more piercing, ear-shattering blasts.

After that he stuck his fingers in his eyes to make tears.

The little devil had disobeyed him.

Cutter was running down the hall toward Jeremy's room.

From the opposite end Cheyenne came flying toward him, her thin white nightgown floating around her body.

Cutter couldn't stop in time.

Neither apparently could she.

Not that he wanted to.

Whatever. They collided.

He wore only pajama bottoms, so his upper body was bare. As she grappled to regain her balance, her hands moved over his naked skin, through his dark, bristly chest hair, across rippling muscle and sinew, burning him.

He wrapped his fingers around her upper arms and jerked her to him, steadying her against his body so she wouldn't fall. He held her so close that each could hear the beat of the other's heart. As he slowly breathed in her warm, dizzying smell, a shiver shot through him. Instantly he was as hard and hot as a brick in an oven. She didn't move away, even though he knew she felt it.

All night he had ached for her. She was made entirely of luscious skin, all soft and warm like smooth, living satin beneath his rough hands. He wanted to go on touching her forever, to lift her gown and slide his hands over every part of her. Her perfumed hair was as fine and light as corn silk where it brushed his cheek and shoulders. Her breasts and hips were alluringly soft and round.

When she stared up at Cutter, he felt consumed by intense, inexplicable emotion. He pulled in a deep breath. It was so good to hold her. It was as if they were the only two people on the planet.

Then Jeremy screamed again.

The kid's yell was damn convincing.

With a worried sigh, her eyes widened and dilated in the dark.

"Jeremy," they whispered in unison.

She with terror. He with annoyance and a trace of amused, fatherly pride.

Reluctantly he let her go. Together they headed into Jeremy's room.

"Jeremy?" she murmured worriedly as she pushed their son's door open.

His bedside lamp chain snapped, and the room was instantly alight. "I'm okay!" croaked Jeremy's cheerful but rather hoarse voice from the bed. "It was just a bad dream."

Jeremy's inky black bangs fell over his brow. His face was white; his eyes red and nervous. Tears streamed down his cheeks.

"My poor darling," she cried.

"I'm okay," Jeremy insisted bravely when she threw her arms around him. He grinned at Cutter. "But—since y'all are both here, maybe you could read me a story or something—"

Mother and son smiled uncertainly at each other and then at Cutter.

Quite naturally, she agreed to a story. Cutter soon found himself enchanted by her soft voice and by Jeremy's eager, rapt expression as he listened to the tale she wove about a little donkey who got lost from his real parents and had only a magic rock to help him find them. Although he sat apart from them, Cutter felt included. For the first time, he almost believed that his dream to be part of a real family might come true. That he and Jeremy and she—

Then it was over and Jeremy had shut his eyes, seemingly asleep.

Her voice died away. She extinguished the light, and the room melted into darkness. For a long moment Cutter and she stared at each other across the dark.

He needed her. As he took her hand and they tiptoed outside together, Cutter prayed that she needed him, too.

Once they were in the hall, Cutter found that when the moment came to release her hand, he couldn't let go of her.

He didn't have to.

Lightning crashed.

Thunder reverberated through the house, and she threw herself into his arms.

"Cutter?" She clutched him tightly.

Slowly he looked down at her.

In the darkness her wide eyes locked on his again.

He pressed her fingertips as if to release them.

She bit her lip and squeezed his hand.

"No," she whispered at last, her voice endearing and small. "Don't leave me."

His words on the beach to her when he'd thought he might die.

The hot look she gave him then made him shiver.

His heart began to beat very fast. "Cheyenne?"

"Truce?" she murmured. "I'm sorry for accusing you—"

"Don't—"

He knew what she wanted, and he didn't intend to make her beg for it.

She begged anyway.

"Please forgive me. Oh, Cutter...touch me. Just hold me." She reached up and trailed trembling fingertips across his cheek, then down the cords of his neck to his shoulder, then still lower over the rigid planes of his chest where they lingered. "I couldn't sleep tonight...because you weren't there to hold me."

"Neither could I—my darling."

"What are you saying?"

"Only this."

A half groan, half laugh escaped him as he hauled her closer and cradled her face in his hands.

As he lowered his mouth, he registered the depth of emotion shining in her eyes.

Then he kissed her.

"Yes! Yes!"

Jeremy squatted next to his door and listened to the exchange and then the long silence outside in the hall that could only mean one thing—his parents were smooching instead of fighting.

Only when he heard his father and his mother walk together down the hall and their door shutting, did Jeremy relax his grip on Molly Pooh and sleepily rub his eyes.

He wondered if they'd kiss some more. Maybe in their bed.

"Yuck."

But he was smiling as he raced with Molly Pooh back to his bed.

Ten

Jack West pulled up on the reins and adjusted his Stetson so he could get a better look at them through the curling heat waves.

Cheyenne looked good. Real good. Neat and sexy and as slim as ever in her black silk sheath.

Her rich husband looked sort of uneasy. *Real* uneasy. Like monsters were chasing him.

Jack West never gave a living soul a second chance.

But he played by different rules when it came to the dead.

Which was why he had taken time away from roundup to ride his great sorrel stallion over to pay his respects to Ivory Rose.

Jack was half-Mexican, half-Anglo, and a lot of prejudiced folks on *El Atascadero* thought less of him for that. His olive skin and inky hair that grew with wild, wayward thickness were several shades darker than most Anglos. His long, muscular body was a shade taller than most Mexicans. There was a dangerous, brooding quality about him that scared people. Cheyenne said that it was his nose, once broken, that gave him the hard, virile look of violence that so unsettled people.

Now, as he stared intently at the little group clustered around Ivory's grave in the shade of the live oak in the cowboy cemetery, his insides churned.

He had to squint a bit and wipe the sweat from his brow to make sure it was really *her*.

So—*Cheyenne had come back*.

Jack had avoided her all the other times.

She shouldn't have come.

Not even for her mother's funeral.

She should be running for her life.

There was a price on her head.

On her rich husband's and kid's, too.

Chantal had told him that some super-rich, border gangster was after them.

Word was they had been boarding a plane to France when Ivory died.

That was just like Ivory. Ornery to her last breath.

Cheyenne and Cutter should have kept on running. Which was probably why Lord kept casting those glances over his shoulder.

Jack's fists balled as he remembered the final conversation he'd had with Chantal. She'd laughed when she'd told him that the monster who'd killed Martin was going after Cheyenne—and her son, too.

"And how would you be knowing that?"

"I'm her sister." Chantal had smiled nervously in that evil, knowing way that could scare even him.

"First time I ever heard you claim kin to her," he'd taunted.

Cheyenne, who was standing apart from her husband and son, looked Jack's way, saw him for the first time and smiled.

Jack froze.

He'd hurt her. He still hated himself for sacrificing their love on the twin altars of greed and lust. But the ranch would be his someday now. At least he had his daughter.

When Cheyenne kept smiling at him, as though she'd forgiven him for what he couldn't forgive himself, Jack remembered his manners. Forcing a wary smile, he tipped his Stetson. Not to be outdone, Salvavidas snorted and pawed the earth.

Jack rode the big horse up to the gate of the cemetery and dismounted. After tying Salvavidas, he began the slow walk up the hill. At the top, he took time to pick at a thick clump of lantana blooming under an ebony tree.

He held the golden blossoms to his nose. Their woodsy scent and Cheyenne's presence brought back the sweet times they'd shared as children. They hadn't wasted much time in front of television sets. Instead they'd ridden bikes and galloped horses across the prairies. They'd picked flowers and run wild and free through the grasses. They'd swum in the creek when the water had been up. He remembered how she used to talk to animals and birds, even snakes in that magical way. How wild things had come to her and eaten out of her hand. How she had talked to plants, too, so that they grew to enormous heights.

Jack put his memories aside and strode toward the small group by the grave. With his white shirt sweat-stained and glued to a strip of skin that ran the length of his lean, muscular back, with his ragged jeans and chaps caked with grime, he wasn't dressed for a funeral.

The preacher was just finishing up as Jack knelt and laid his bright yellow flowers on the dark, gleaming coffin.

After the service, Jack was stunned when the first person to approach Cheyenne was Theodora. He was further stunned when she invited Cheyenne and her family to *El Atascadero* for refreshments.

Cheyenne smiled hesitantly before taking his mother-in-law's thin hand.

Theodora smiled, too. The gossips began to buzz when slowly the two women turned and took the first step on that long walk toward the big house together.

It was about time.

Ben West's other daughter, his best daughter, had finally come home.

Not back to her mother's shack in the swamp.

But home to *El Atascadero*, her father's home.

Where she had always belonged.

They should be on a jet right now. Not in Texas, riding around on shoulderless blacktopped, county roads in this heat.

"There!" Cheyenne suddenly cried as a shabby cedar roof loomed above tangled branches of a clump of mesquite and salt cedar that grew dangerously close to the road. "That's it! Turn-n-n—here!"

Cutter wrenched the steering wheel hard to the right. The car swerved, its engine snarling as if it were a bad-tempered cat as the car jounced onto the narrow, potholed shell driveway that led to Ivory's shack.

Maybe it was the heat. Maybe he was just tired from a long day filled with senseless delays and fruitless sentimentality. Whatever. Such emotional craziness was what Cutter had feared when he'd tried to talk Cheyenne out of attending her mother's funeral.

Didn't she realize they were going to be murdered if they didn't clear out and fast?

It was just before twilight.

The air was warm and humid, the huge sky a soft, glowing lavender above wide-open, brown pastures. A white mist clung to the ground near the marshes behind Ivory's shack. When Cutter braked, whorls of dust curled around the car.

It wasn't hard to see where the mantle of grime that lay on top the two, ancient, rusted pickups that had died in the driveway had come from. Both vehicles had smashed windshields. They had no tires and were propped on cement blocks. Waist-high weeds and cacti surrounded the house and cars. A pair of feral, black cats slunk from the porch. When they vanished into the weeds, he felt their eyes watching him. Other eyes, too.

Ivory had only been dead two days. Yet, her house already seemed dead as well. The wind made eerie, rustling sounds in the branches of the squat oaks and in the long shadowy grasses behind the house. A broken shutter slammed back and forth against a wall.

He and Cheyenne should be clearing out—before it got darker. Before José sent who-knew-how-many villains after them.

But there was no talking sense to her. She was determined to give him the local tour of her childhood.

Hell, maybe this guilt trip was about his not letting her come sooner. Whatever. She had been in this strange, desolate mood ever since she'd found out her mother was dead. He had tried to comfort her, but her black mood had only worsened after her mother's coffin had been lowered into the ground and Theodora had welcomed her into her daddy's house as if she was a long-lost daughter.

"I'm Ivory's daughter," Cheyenne had repeated guiltily to him as Theodora had led them across thick, plush carpets, down long halls into showy drawing rooms of Ben's vast mansion. "Not Theodora's. I want you to know that."

Now, in the fading light, Cheyenne fearfully studied her mother's dilapidated house and then searched his face.

"Okay," he said. "We're here. You've shown it to me. Now, can we go?"

Cheyenne turned to him; her face ashen, her eyes brilliant and charged. "This is where I grew up. My mother was Ivory Rose, the witch woman. She skinned rattlesnakes and made hat bands out of their hides. She collected bird eggs, pierced and drained them, painted them, and gave them to the *vaqueros'* children to wear as necklaces. She could pick up a snake by the neck and charm it to sleep." Cheyenne flung the car door open and raced up the driveway.

He jumped out. "Why are you doing this, when you know we're in danger—"

"Because I want you to see this. To know exactly who I am. I wasn't raised in my father's mansion." She paused.

Her green eyes dilated with pain. "You didn't think I was good enough back when you first heard of me—"

"I'm sorry for that. Sorrier than you'll ever know. But that was a long time ago. We really should go," Cutter insisted, quickening and lengthening his strides so that he could catch her. "The sooner we get out of here, honey, the better. Hernando—"

The warm swamp mists enveloped them. Cicadas sang from an oak mott. Unseen animals splashed in the dark ponds hidden by the tall reeds. Behind the house rosemary and other herbs had gone wild and grown to magical heights.

She opened a screen door that had innumerable small holes and tears. He got a whiff of the vile stench of cats.

"You have to see this first," she pleaded in that same stricken tone. "This is the worst house anywhere for miles around Westville. People used to say it was haunted even when Mother was still alive. The few kids that would play with me at school were afraid to play here."

"Cheyenne, baby, you've got to forget all that—"

"No. You've got to forget Hernando for a second and listen to me." Her voice was quivering now. "I've been running from this place and my childhood all my life. You followed me to the island because you didn't think I was good enough to marry Martin. Well, neither did I. I probably would never have dated him, if growing up here, and being thought the trashiest and wildest girl in town, hadn't given me the neurotic need to prove—"

"Cheyenne, darling, stop it—"

"Don't you see?" she pleaded. "Martin might never have felt he had to borrow that money, if money and its trappings hadn't been so important to me."

Cutter didn't feel up to this. "Look. Ambition is usually fueled by neurotic needs. Mine was. Forget the past. Now isn't the time—"

"No." With a shaking hand she pointed to a trellis from which the thick black tatters of a dead vine hung. "I used to climb that. I'd sit up on the roof all night long when

Mama had some new cowboy lover here. The stars and moon would seem so close and bright...sometimes I'd stand up and try to touch them. A bunch of buzzards used to roost every night in that mesquite tree, so I never felt all that alone even though sometimes it was nearly dawn before I came down and went inside. You probably didn't know that buzzards are real friendly creatures. Friendlier at least than most small town kids who've been taught by decent folk to hate you."

"Cheyenne—"

"I was so ashamed. Some nights I wanted to stay out on the roof forever. I didn't want to hear them making love. I vowed that when I grew up, I would do things so differently. I swore my child wouldn't ever have to grow up feeling ashamed of who he was or who I was. I was going to live in a house grander than my daddy's, too. Most of all, my child would have a daddy. That's why I married—" Her frightened voice fell away.

He suddenly knew why she'd had to marry Martin.

To protect her child.

No. To protect their child.

"What a laugh," she whispered. "I made an even bigger mess of my life than she did of hers. Every time Martin and I fought, Jeremy would go out and climb a tree. Then I got Jeremy kidnapped."

The porch was steamingly hot, as though it still held all the heat of the day, and yet Cutter scarcely felt it. All he saw was the helpless, scared look in Cheyenne's eyes.

"I wish you could have known her," she said.

"I do, too."

"Do you really mean that?"

"Yes." Gently Cutter took her by the hand. "Honey, let's go."

She clutched his fingers tightly, tugging him closer.

"What the hell are you so afraid of, Cheyenne?"

"Just, just come inside. This is very important to me. To us."

He cast a backward glance over his shoulder as she led him inside.

All the windows were closed, and the hot rooms reeked of musty, sick-room smells. He felt an aching inside him when she showed him her pitifully tiny bedroom.

Mice had made a nest in one corner. As he studied the scribblings of happy faces she'd made on the wallpaper as a child and the dusty bookshelves stacked with used, paperback thrillers, he remembered the vast mansions of many floors and much privacy that he'd grown up in.

"I think you turned out pretty well," he said.

Silently she led him into her mother's bedroom.

He opened a window, but the fresh air could do little toward dispelling the sickening odors that had been accumulating for weeks.

Outside it was getting dark fast.

Anybody could see the car.

Ivory's house was a trap.

As if in a trance, Cheyenne stood at the foot of the bed, staring at the bare mattress, no doubt imagining Ivory lying there still. No doubt feeling guilty she hadn't been with her at the end.

"Nobody thought she was much of a mother. She got all my clothes out of barrels at the church that were other kids' castoffs. She never made me take a bath or wash my hair or brush my teeth like other moms. I could stay up to dawn if I wanted to. I could sleep out in the woods or wherever else I wanted. I could wear what I wanted or run around buck naked. I could eat cake and drink sodas for breakfast every day. I had way too much freedom, and everyone disapproved of me. Even Maverick, Chantal's cousin. Everybody except Jack...at least till Chantal got to him, too. You see, Chantal was always somewhere in the background, making me feel like I was dirt with just a few well-chosen words about me or my mother. You don't know what it was like, having a sister like her. Terrible things happened to me at school. But Ivory wasn't so bad," Cheyenne murmured. "I loved her. She loved me."

If that were so, maybe Cheyenne had had more than he'd had growing up in his parents' mansions. People were what counted. Relationships. He wanted some strong, loving relationships in his life. He wanted her.

"We have to go," he repeated.

"When you came to the island because you thought I was no good, you probably didn't guess by a long shot what a lowlife I really was." She turned to him. "Well, now you know. I was wild and bad and poor— So poor, Jack, who was poor, too, chose Chantal over me even though he didn't think much of her. So wild...I didn't take his rejection like a lady."

"Shhhhh—"

Suddenly he realized why she was so afraid.

A guilty flush crept up his neck. It was his fault she had so little faith in him. His fault she thought the cabin would make him despise her and reject her again.

They stared into each other's eyes. For a long moment neither of them spoke; neither moved.

His heart began to slam in slow, painful strokes.

He loved her.

"Cheyenne." His voice was quiet and deep. "Do you really think I give a damn about any of this now?"

"Well, you used to. You disapproved of me just like everybody did around here. You thought I was easy. Trash. Somebody you could have sex with and leave pregnant. I—I loved you. I really loved you. I thought I would die when you didn't come back."

Tears began to spill down her cheeks.

He had never known someone else's pain could hurt so much.

"When you didn't come back I knew you hated me just like everybody did here."

"No. It didn't happen that way."

She was so beautiful in black, with her flaming hair and pale oval face. As he gazed down at her, his own eyes grew dazed and unfocused as he realized the extent of her pain and fear and hurt. Her lovely face began to blur.

"I—I shouldn't have said these things to you," she whispered. "I—I want too much. Things a girl like me can't ever hope to—"

He caught the scent of her, and it was alluringly warm and fragrant. His emotions were so bafflingly deep and profound that his heart began to slam against his rib cage. "No—"

"I don't expect you to care about me. Not really. I just wanted you to know why I was so afraid of being poor, of feeling ashamed for the rest of my life— But none of that is important to me now. I just wish I could have been with her when—" She tried to push past him and run from the house.

"Cheyenne. I do care." He wrapped his arms around her, squeezing her against himself, crushing her, her damp cheek against the heavy pounding rhythm of his heart. "Honey," he whispered, beginning in a rush. "I loved you, too. From the minute I saw you, I must've loved you. I still do, and I always will. I guess I just didn't know how to say it till now. Nothing else matters. Not Martin. Not this house. Not your mother. I don't care how you grew up. I'm glad you loved her."

Gently he kissed her.

She was trembling.

Suddenly so was he.

"I love you," he repeated. "I loved you that first day on the beach. I always will."

"Why didn't you ever say it then?"

"Maybe everything happened too fast. Maybe I just didn't know how. Maybe I thought you could tell how I felt. I didn't deliberately make you pregnant and leave you. I always wanted you and Jeremy. You have to believe that."

She looked up at him—very, very slowly, studying every single one of his features in one of those suspended moments in time. "I—I guess I do. I really do. And I love you, too," she whispered at long last. "I love you."

And as she said it, he found the courage to say it to her again. And again. "I love you. I love you—"

Years of frustration and pain flowed out of him. Out of her, too.

Desire overtook him.

He forgot José.

Nothing mattered but his fierce pagan need to have her and to show her how much he cared.

He began to kiss her.

First her warm, silken throat. Then her mouth.

The outer lips. And inside them, too.

She melted.

His passion escalated.

So did hers.

The rapidly increasing throb of his chest grew in tempo with the mad beat of her heart. Within seconds he had her up against the wall again, their lower bodies joined. Impatiently he yanked her black silk dress above her thighs and his fly apart so he could plant himself inside her.

He was too hard and too fast.

It was over too soon.

And yet afterward as they stared at each other in that steamy darkness of their own making, their bodies drenched with perspiration, their sticky clothes a twisted tangle at their hips, there was a new understanding as well as a new tenderness between them.

Fierce and quick as their mating had been, more than lust had been involved. It had been a mating of their souls and minds and hearts as well. It had held the beginning of true trust and long-lasting love.

Still, when they could breathe again, he gently cupped her chin, meaning to apologize for his roughness. ·

But she sealed his lips with a fingertip.

"No—"

"I—I—"

"Don't spoil it." Her voice was soft and a little wondrous. Her eyes gentle and hot. "You said you loved me, and I knew you meant it. It was wonderful." She blushed. "Too wonderful for words. And sometimes I'll want it like that again."

Eleven

Cutter stared at the slowly turning blades of the ceiling fan and yawned, his mood that of utter boredom.

Then a bolt of sheer-white lightning zigzagged from the low scudding clouds to the forest floor, jolted him out of his mood and startled the flock of parrots that had been chattering gaily in the nearby palms. Green wings fanned as they swooped from their perches, swooshing past the cabana with its crimson and purple cascades of bougainvillea to some perch of greater safety in the rain forest.

The sun that had sparkled harshly on the bay all afternoon vanished in an instant. The sky was rapidly blackening; the still, humid sea air freshening. Seconds later the huge fanlike leaves of the banana trees and palms began to whip against the screened windows of the cabana. Thunder rumbled.

At least now there would be a storm to watch.

Not wanting to wake Cheyenne, Cutter carefully got out of bed. Tugging on the pair of jeans he found on the floor and slipping into a white, long-sleeved shirt, he stepped out onto the balcony, intending to watch the storm.

A dozen pink orchids blazed from a bowl on the table by the wicker rocker. Only that morning he had picked them from a field that he and Cheyenne visited every morning.

Three weeks.

They had been trapped in this remote hellhole for three damn weeks.

He heard Jeremy who'd made friends with some other kids shout from the pool when heavy tropical raindrops began pelting the tin roof and palm fronds. In the next instant the sweet, wet scent of rain permeated everything. The boys got out of the pool and dashed for shelter in a nearby cabana.

Rain again.

Damn.

Down here it was like turning on a faucet.

Sheets of rain began streaming from the tin roof into the gutters.

Costa Rica.

Land of beautiful travel posters.

Land of orchids and coffee plantations.

Land of mountain ranges, arid desert, seacoasts and resorts on both the Pacific and the Atlantic.

Land of unending jungle with washed-out dirt roads and electric green foliage, land of actively smoldering volcanoes, swampy marshlands, dark, impenetrable fogs and ferocious, never-ceasing rains. At least, they were ferocious during the rainy season.

The Costa Ricans were as mild as their habitat was violent. They had one expression to cover the multitude of unpleasant conditions, which their climate forced upon them, and that was *pura vida.* When it rained and wouldn't stop, they would sigh and say, *pura vida.* When a plane couldn't take off for days because of fog, they said *pura vida.*

One gorgeous sunny day Cutter had rented their simple cabana on a hill because its balconies overlooked dense green jungle and a stunningly blue Pacific.

Manuel Antonio National Park.

The park had been touted as one of the world's most beautiful, undeveloped paradises. It had lush green mountains covered with dense rain forests. A cool stream even flowed over the beach and emptied into the bathwater-calm ocean. The rain forest was inhabited by orange-and-purple crabs, three-toed tree sloths, iguanas and chipper squirrel monkeys. The snorkeling was great. So were the sunsets.

When she'd first stepped out onto the balcony of the cabana and seen the beach, Cheyenne had sworn to him that she would never tire of the spectacular views.

He, who'd never given a damn for views, who didn't like being cut off from civilization, had grown mortally sick of everything in an hour.

Cheyenne, who was more a beach person and nature person and a swimmer than he, who as a shell seeker loved to get up at dawn and prowl for shells, who loved exploring the rain forest with its exotic flora and fauna, had been maddeningly enthusiastic at first. She had shrieked with delight at every alstroemeria, anthurium, colorful crab or sloth. She had been dazzled by the thousands of varieties of orchids growing in a field near their cabana. But now, she was as sick of it all as he was. Jeremy, however, liked Costa Rica. He felt safe and was rapidly healing from the trauma of his kidnapping.

Still, three weeks of black beans and rice and gallo pinto had them all yearning for American food. Three weeks of being cut off from his businesses had Cutter feeling bored and restless.

Cutter had chosen Costa Rica as the place to hide because his first instinct had been to flee to Indonesia or France. It was Paul who had advised him to pick a less obvious place.

"Other than Mexico, the very last place Hernando would think you'd choose is some country in Central America."

"I don't have any businesses down there or even any friends."

"My point exactly," Paul had persisted. "And neither does Hernando."

"I still prefer Europe."

"Costa Rica is supposed to be the Switzerland of Central America. It doesn't even have an army. Like I said, Hernando never sets foot there."

Cutter had reluctantly sent his corporate jet, three look-alike decoys posing as himself, Cheyenne, and Jeremy, along with Paul O'Connor to the south of France to lay a trap for Hernando at Cutter's seaside villa. Cutter had then had false passports made for the three of them to come to Costa Rica. They were passing themselves off as an executive and family who needed to study Spanish before he took a job in Argentina.

Jeremy had balked at all the Spanish, so Cutter enrolled him in karate lessons in an attempt to restore his confidence. The lessons had been in Spanish, but Jeremy had kicked and chopped with the best of the other kids.

The posh language school in the center of San José had lasted a mere week.

Bad idea.

It had been impossible for Cutter to concentrate on Spanish when he'd constantly been on the lookout for Hernando. All three of them had quickly tired of San José and its bad buses, smog and terrible traffic. Not to mention the endless grammar lessons. Besides, Cutter had been easily spooked in the crowded city. On several occasions when they'd picked Jeremy up at karate, Cutter had been almost sure someone was following them. So, he'd decided a remote jungle cabana cut off from the more populated parts of the country by mountains and impassable dirt roads would be a better hiding place.

The phone buzzed from the sitting room.

He dashed back inside and caught it.

"Lord. O'Connor here."

Usually Paul used first names and at least said hello. Why was he so damned formal all of a sudden?

"Lord—"

Heavy bursts of static broke up Paul's tense voice.

"You'll have to speak up. We've got a bad connection."

"We've got him. You're safe. You can come home."

Cutter wanted more than terse generalities. He needed details. "Paul, how the devil did you manage—"

Lightning crashed, and Paul's voice exploded in static. Then there was silence.

"Paul—" Cutter yelled.

Nothing.

Not even a damned dial tone.

Miserable country.

Feeling frustrated but elated, too, Cutter set the phone down and went back out to watch the rain.

The storm no longer seemed so oppressive. In the morning, or whenever the rain stopped, maybe some time in the next century, he thought cynically, they could leave.

Paul had Hernando.

Cutter couldn't believe it had been so easy.

Cutter heard a sound from the bedroom. Next he caught the murmur of light, fluid footsteps as Cheyenne padded across the tile floor and opened the balcony door.

"What are you doing out there?" she whispered.

He turned. "Watching the rain."

"Bored again?" she teased, mussing her red hair with her fingers.

He found himself feasting on the shower of thick burning auburn as it tumbled against her slim white throat and creamy shoulders. She was wearing an ivory cotton gown, cut low and made of gauzy stuff that was revealingly transparent. Just looking at her brought such pleasure that he found himself feasting on the curve of her breasts and pouting nipples.

She had asked if he was bored.

"Not now."

She blushed. "Who called?"

"Paul. With good news."

"He's got him?"

"Yes."

Her face lit up. "You mean—"

"We're safe."

"I can't believe it."

His muscles tensed. "Cheyenne, we can go home."

Her green eyes seemed very large; her lips very wet. "I just can't believe it."

Neither could he. But he didn't tell her that. "You are so beautiful."

"Say it," she whispered, slightly breathless now, coming nearer. "I want to hear it again, right now, now that we're safe and everything is really going to be all right."

"I thought you'd be sick of hearing it."

"No. Say it again."

This demand of hers had become a sacred ritual and part of their mating dance.

The rain had become a torrential downpour. It was falling in drenching sheets, pounding the corrugated roof of their cabana, gushing down the metal gutters and out the spouts. Slick, wet curtains surrounded them. The road to the beach was a river.

For once he didn't care. Being with her on the balcony was like standing in the middle of a waterfall. Suddenly, as the gleaming curtains of water roared around them, he found the view very beautiful.

"I love you," he whispered. "I don't give a damn if you were born poor. I didn't come back...just for Jeremy. I came back for you. I should have told you that—from the first."

Humid mists from the rain enveloped them. Her white gown grew damp and began to stick to her body, so that she looked sexier than ever.

Why was it they always seemed to be making love in the rain?

"Again," she insisted, licking a droplet of spray from her lips.

"I love you. Only you, Cheyenne. Forever. Always."

"A-g-gain—" she drawled playfully, Texas style, coming toward him, her hips undulating.

"When you married Martin, I thought I'd die."

"I loved only you even then," she confessed. "Only you. All those years. Even when I thought you hated me."

"We were such fools."

Her face seemed to go pale in the shadowy gray light. God, what eyes she had! he thought, great melting dark green eyes that made him lose his soul. Not that she hadn't always possessed it.

"A-gain—" she pleaded.

She stood within inches of him now.

The pulse in his throat had begun beating very fast. Her mere nearness was enough to send him over the edge.

"There's only one way to end this game," he growled huskily, seizing her, kissing her savagely.

Her lips parted immediately.

And soon he couldn't stop.

He was glad Jeremy was gone and couldn't possibly get back home in this downpour. The cabana was terribly small, he realized as he lifted her and carried her inside. The walls suddenly seemed to press in on them. After all it was only four tiny rooms linked by a hall.

As he lowered her to their bed, he knew that it had never been like this with anybody before. He had never felt so hot, so crazily involved with any woman.

She was his wife. The mother of his child.

Ever since he'd first declared his love for her in her mother's shack, Cutter had been possessed by love. Every time they did it, the sex got hotter, and his feelings grew deeper.

He wanted to kiss her for a long time, to explore her mouth, to draw out their lovemaking. But her fingers were tearing his shirt apart and pulling the zipper of his jeans down.

She was hungry. Too hungry to wait.

Still kissing her, Cutter lifted her gown and tore it off. Soon their garments dripped from the end of the bed and littered the floor. They lay together on top of the sheets, he savoring the slick warmth of her naked curves, she the rough texture of the black whorls of hair that covered his chest. She tried to speak, but his mouth closed over hers. Hushing her, he fused their bodies together.

Her arms came around his neck, her lips trembling beneath his as his passion raged out of control and swept them ever deeper into a wild, dark storm that was all their own.

Afterward, when it was over, they lay quietly, their arms circling each other as they listened to the hammering rain. From time to time she stirred against him, but only to nestle closer under the sheets and blankets or to brush her lips against his cheek.

He loved her.

And she loved him.

They were safe.

At last.

The warm, sweet night rain swirled around the cabana and cut them off from the world. In that moment Costa Rica seemed almost a paradise.

He fell asleep again, thinking the danger was over, that they could go home in the morning, that never again would he hear the annoying words, *pura vida*, that they would be together forever.

That they would live happily ever after like couples in fairy tales.

Some time during the night they both awoke to a nightmare at the very same instant. They held each other until they fell asleep again.

Later he woke up again to the rumble of a plane flying low over the dark, rain-swept jungle.

Unable to believe that anybody could be fool enough to fly in weather like this, Cutter went back to sleep.

His first inkling of danger was when he awoke alone, and it was noon.

Sunshine was blasting into the empty cabana.

Someone was banging on the door.

But Cheyenne was gone.

Twelve

As Cheyenne studied the two-mile crescent of utterly deserted, white sand, she felt happy. Happier than she'd ever been.

Not because she was the first shell seeker and she had the beach all to herself.

Nor because there was no better time to look for shells than after a storm.

No. Cheyenne felt that singular sparkling happiness of a woman who knew at last that she was well loved. She couldn't stop thinking of Cutter and their night of steamy passion. She kept remembering the way he had looked as he'd lain sleeping this morning with his hooded eyes closed and his luxuriant black hair crisp and dark against the white pillow. For a long while she had stood beside the bed, savoring his carved profile. Then she'd watched the gentle rise and fall of his massive, bronzed chest and remembered how virile and strong he'd seemed when he'd wrapped her in his arms and pressed his body into hers. She had taken pleasure that he looked younger and more relaxed this morning than he ever had before. That the cynical lines on either side of his sensual mouth had all but vanished. That he had looked almost happy and at peace, as if what they had shared together meant everything to him.

Last night had been the first time that they had made love without fear. Without dread of José.

She closed her eyes, remembering all the things Cutter had done to her, remembering how his tongue had dipped inside her navel, how he had held her down, how his hands had roamed over her until he'd thoroughly aroused her. He had told her he loved her dozens of times, in dozens of ways. He'd shown her, too.

All her life she had been starved for love, and this bright morning was the first that she could look forward to sharing her future with the man she loved and who loved her.

Blushing, she pushed her wanton, but much-cherished memories from her mind. Then she lifted her white skirts above her slender ankles and ran lightly across the lagoon. Once she reached high, dry sand on the other side, she stood there, listening to the peaceful lapping of the surf at the shore.

In the golden darkness she could see the shadows of the fishing boats anchored offshore. One of them was a huge Cigarette boat, which she hadn't seen before. Some rich tourist perhaps.

The park was officially closed. Usually she came here in the afternoon with Cutter and Jeremy and the other tourists. Jeremy loved the iguanas that ventured shyly out of the jungle onto the beach because they reminded him of the dinosaurs in *Jurassic Park,* his favorite movie. She usually swam a mile or two while he and Cutter read or explored the sea caves. She loved it here, especially now that she felt safe. The scene before her was quiet, peaceful—normal, like her life was going to be.

Millions of shells littered the beach.

As she ran toward them, she knew that even though the danger was past, Cutter wouldn't have let her come alone if he'd been awake.

As she leaned down and gathered her first glistening,

pearly treasure, she told herself she'd be back in bed long before he ever knew she had gone.

As she picked up another shell, a small black shape suddenly flashed across the beach.

She stopped to watch as a white-faced monkey raced into the jungle.

Something had scared it.

As she studied the silent wall of palms and mangrove trees that ran parallel to the beach, a nearby snake, sensing some unseen danger, slithered from beneath the gnarled tangle of mangrove roots into the black jungle.

Something gleamed from the trees. For no reason at all the vision seemed sinister. She blinked once, and then squinted, but whatever had been there, was gone.

The sun went behind a cloud, and a strange, cold wind swept across the cove without making a ripple on the water. Then it gusted up the beach and tore through the rain forest. Suddenly, like a wild creature, she, too, sensed an alien dangerous presence.

The wind died.

Once again the rain forest loomed dense and dark, like an impenetrable wall, imprisoning her. As she watched and listened, the dark green fringe of jungle grew quieter.

Too quiet.

Suddenly the beach with its glistening shells felt too deserted and lonely for her to enjoy her solitary walk.

Spooked, she began edging back toward the lagoon and the road on the other side of it, retracing her steps.

A monkey howled from the trees, its shrill solitary voice a warning.

Shivering, she rubbed her bare arms and told herself she was being ridiculous.

She forced herself to kneel down and pick up another shell.

But this one was black and gritty and ugly. When she turned it over, it disintegrated in her hands and an ugly creature that looked as deadly as a scorpion skittered out of it.

It was a sign.

She screamed, and throwing down the shell, she ran.

She couldn't see him.

But she could feel his dark, unseen force in the shadowy jungle as she raced back toward the shallow lagoon.

But the sand was so deep, she was soon exhausted.

With her every step, her bare feet seemed to sink more deeply into the ankle-deep sand. He stalked her remorselessly as he raced along the hard, packed path that lay just inside the jungle.

Sweaty and too light-headed to go on, she stopped before she was halfway to the lagoon. Her chest was heaving, and she had to gasp for every breath.

He stopped, too.

When she could breathe again, she decided the straightest path to the cabana was through the jungle.

Two minutes later she was plunging through thick canopies of dark vines, and then through a long tunnel of overarching palms.

The rain forest was dark and quiet. It was like entering a cathedral and leaving the real world behind. Fearing snakes or iguanas, she, nevertheless, sank down into a thick bed of damp ferns to rest a minute.

The trees with their dripping ivies and lacy ferns were so shadowy and all-enveloping that she considered hiding there indefinitely. Then she made out the shape of a howler monkey, ambling toward her along the narrow trail. Overhead more monkeys kept up with him by racing from branch to branch.

Strange how the monkeys made no sound.

Strange how the figure on the trail kept growing larger and larger—until he was much too large to be a monkey.

With a chill she realized that her monkey was a man, and that the man was walking steadily and deliberately toward her. She felt that he knew she was there, that he had known all along, that he knew he had all the time in the world to take her.

Her dress was white.

In another instant he would be so close he couldn't miss her.

She bolted away from him, running headlong down the path of overhanging darkness that led away from the sunny road and the swimming pool and the cabanas. Away from Cutter.

Her pursuer raced after her.

When her pace slowed, his did, too.

But he was breathing so hard she could hear him.

When she glanced back over her shoulder to see how close he was, she stumbled on a sprawling root and fell.

Her head hit a tree. Then she was on the ground, and the dense trees were blackening.

Something wet was dripping on her cheek. She opened her eyes to blurred shadows and radiant green foliage. Less than a foot away, a twig snapped under a heavy boot heel.

Dear God. She gasped in panic as an ever-tightening band of fear compressed her lungs.

He took a final step, so that when she tried to lever herself to a sitting position, her fingers touched the dusty toes of his tall, black leather boots.

From her vantage point on the jungle floor, her gaze traveled up his muscular legs, widening in shock when she registered his swarthy features.

"Get up, *señora*."

She had never seen him before. Still, from Cutter's description, she recognized him instantly.

"*Mucho gusto, señora*. My name is José Hernando."

His raspy voice was so ordinary. As was his face. His broad Indian nose, his olive dark eyes and swarthy skin were the features of so many Costa Ricans. Even his thin, cruel lips, so like a Spanish conquistador's, were common enough, too. Had she chanced to meet him elsewhere, she would never have known him for a killer.

"How did you find us?"

"Your sister."

"Chantal?"

"I met her the night of your auction. We became friends." He smiled. "More than friends. She is a woman of extraordinary talents." He spoke in a cold, dispassionate tone. "She knew you would go to your mother's funeral. She followed you to Costa Rica and called me. Funny, I was in Europe. I never considered this a possible hiding place. I suppose it's a nice country—if you don't mind the rain."

In a panic, Cheyenne tried to crawl away, but Hernando stamped his boot down, nailing her to the damp earth with her skirt. Then he pulled her up by her hair.

"Cutter," she whispered in a desperate, frozen voice.

"He can't help you now."

So, it had all been for nothing.

Their marriage.

Their love.

Their happiness.

Everything.

Thirteen

When the door of the cabana crashed open, Cutter bolted awake instantly. He knew at once that Cheyenne was gone and that he had a dangerous intruder.

Cutter was diving for his pistol in the bedside table, as Hernando burst into the bedroom with Cheyenne, an arm braced across her shoulder, his hand around her throat in a viselike grip, his automatic weapon drawn.

"Don't even think about it, *bastardo*."

The undertone in Hernando's voice sent a chill through Cutter. He let his hand fall limply away from the drawer. No way could he risk a shot with Hernando using Cheyenne as a shield.

"*Buenos días, mi amigo.* This time I have your queen. So—it's checkmate. I win. You lose."

Cheyenne's cry was low-throated, fearfully guilty. "Cutter, I'm sorry I went out without—"

"Shut up—" Hernando growled.

She swallowed convulsively as Hernando's hand tightened on her throat.

Cutter's head jerked toward her. Her skin was chalk

white; her enormous eyes were wide with fright. Seeing her like that filled Cutter with revulsion. Her white dress was torn and muddy. There were bruises on her neck and face.

The bastard had put his hands on her, mauled her, hurt her. Hell. Who knew what else?

Hernando's eyes burned like coals as he shoved the barrel of his gun hard into her cheek. "Now, smart guy, sweat! Crawl! Pray!" He waved his gun. "Get down on the floor! Now! On your knees! Then beg me for her life, or I'll shoot her now!" He moved the gun back to her face. "Then you'll die, too. And I'll tell the world that the great *el genio* is a wimp without *huevos*."

Cutter felt utter, blinding rage. The muscles in his face tightened into a savage mask of hate. "Let her go. You can have anything you want. Only let her go."

"Where's the boy?"

The two men glared at each other in the jarring stillness of the tiny cabana. The only sounds were the steamy dripping of rainwater from the eaves and the incessant chatter of the parrots from the nearby trees.

"Where is he?" Hernando yelled.

"Let go of my mom, pervert!" Jeremy screamed from a back window.

When Hernando whirled, Cutter dived for his enemy's knees.

Jeremy's dark head disappeared from the window.

"Call him back!" Hernando howled as Cutter crushed his right knee and a bone cracked.

"Let her go, or I'll tear out your larynx!"

Just as Cutter slammed a fist into Hernando's jaw, the gun exploded.

"Jeremy!" Cutter cried out. "Cheyenne! Run! Meet me at the field of orchids! If one of us doesn't make it, don't come back, no matter—"

Hernando fired again. Cutter's voice died away as blood spurted from his shoulder. He could barely feel the bullet that had ripped through bone and sinew as he sagged weakly to the floor.

* * *

A third bullet shattered glass.

Orchids and water spilled everywhere and mingled with Cutter's blood.

Miraculously the hard hands at Cheyenne's throat fell away. Hernando was hugging his knee. The next thing she knew Jeremy was dragging her free and pulling her out of the cabana into the jungle to safety. Cutter staggered up and was right behind them as they raced from the cabana through snarled tangles of foliage and dripping rain forest.

They tried to stay together as they ran down the familiar path that led to the field of orchids, but Cutter was breathing hard and moved slower. The rain forest was so dense and dark, they were soon separated.

She and Jeremy broke out of the forest and into the sunny field of dazzling pink blossoms at almost the same moment.

But Cutter wasn't there.

They didn't dare scream his name.

When he didn't come, she folded Jeremy, who was as pale as death to her frightened eyes, into her arms. They sank to their knees in the bright, soft-petaled blossoms. Motionless, they clung to each other, hugging each other. She smoothed the black hair from his hot face, waiting and praying silently to herself for another five or ten tense minutes.

Not so long ago all she had wanted was to be free of danger, to have her son. To have her own life.

She had not wanted to marry Cutter.

But everything was different now.

Hernando had kidnapped her son. Traumatized him.

But Cutter had come and gotten Jeremy back. Cutter had helped heal Jeremy and professed his love for her.

Hernando had almost killed her. Now he had Cutter.

She loved Cutter.

He had risked his life to save hers. He was willing to die for her now. He had known he'd been hit, when he'd ordered them not to go back.

But she would have no life without him.

Jeremy would have no father.

Cutter had told her not to come back for him and, in truth, the mere thought of facing Hernando again terrified her. But the thought of what Hernando would do to Cutter if she didn't go was even more shattering.

"Jeremy, baby, I have to go back and try to help your father," she whispered raggedly, starting to rise. "You have to stay here."

"No!" Stubbornly he tugged on her skirt.

"Jeremy, if you go back, too, he'll kill us all. Your father and I don't want that."

"I took karate, didn't I?"

She smiled faintly, hopelessly. "No. Absolutely no. You have to stay here."

"But, Mom, you just sat on the bench and watched me."

"I paid attention," she said bravely. "Stay here. End of argument."

Tiny droplets of blood spattered the jungle floor.

Cutter could barely stand up, much less run.

Still, he staggered forward, panting; what little strength he had left was draining out of him.

His torn shirt was blood-soaked. The boiling-hot pain in his right shoulder was spreading down his arms and spine. He couldn't feel his hands. His legs were paralyzed; his vision was blurred by mists of pain, and his sense of direction obliterated by the tunnel of thick draperies both ahead and behind.

When he fell, he couldn't get up. A terrible cold was creeping through his body. Still, he smiled as he imagined Cheyenne and Jeremy safe, together, in the field of orchids.

He could die happy, if only they were safe.

Cheyenne was all that mattered. She and Jeremy.

All his life he had wanted love.

For a brief, shining time he had found it.

Cutter held that thought even when he heard Hernando stumbling on his bad knee as he tramped through the thick jungle undergrowth, his clumsy, crashing steps growing ever louder.

Cutter imagined *her* face, when she was all aglow after they'd made love.

Cheyenne. He wanted to die with her image branded on his brain.

He saw her on the beach with her glorious red hair blowing in the wind when he would have died if she hadn't saved him. He thought of her eyes, which changed from emerald to hazy green, depending on her mood. He thought of the way they lit up with joy or darkened when he made love to her.

Almost, he could be happy as he lay there and thought of her. Almost.

He shut his eyes and waited for his executioner.

Hernando was at the helm of his Cigarette boat racing out of the cove at incredible speed. There was no anger in him now, only grim pleasure and satisfaction as he roared away from the other fishing boats whose brawny captains and crews waved to him.

Maybe *el genio* had smashed his knee. Maybe he'd even be crippled for life.

But he, Hernando, had won.

His men had made easy work of Lord's man in Cannes and forced him to call his boss and lie. Then they'd beaten O'Connor and dumped him into the Mediterranean. Incredibly the tough bastard had swum to shore and lived.

El genio would die for sure. He would motor farther out.

Too bad he'd passed out cold again and, thereby, was out of his misery. The rich wimp had taken a bullet through his shoulder. He'd bled like a stuck bull, all over the cockpit. He was as white as a phantom and bound and gagged and unconscious now. His ankles were chained to a concrete block. As soon as he reached deep blue water, Hernando would throw him overboard.

Hernando was regretting that the woman and the boy had gotten away when he heard a noise from the cabin. As he turned, he gave a startled cry when *they* sprang at him from the hatch.

The boy and the woman.

His hands fell away from the throttle as they jumped him with stunning force.

The boat raced on at its dizzying speed as he dived for his gun.

He collapsed on his bad knee, and the gun slid away.

Díos! Where had they come from?

She struck a glancing blow to the back of his head. The boy's hand crashed into his neck in a karate chop.

A wave broke across the bow, drenching him. Blinded by salt spray, Hernando lost his grip on the wheel.

The boat spun out of control.

His last thought was, "Good, I will kill them all!"

But she hit him again. A puny blow, but the boat lurched. He fell forward, flailing his arms, unable to get away from her. His forehead crashed into the windshield.

The boat rolled. His good leg buckled, and he went reeling to starboard. Blinded, off balance, he grabbed at everything, anything, wanting to take the boy and the woman with him as he fell.

His hand locked in a vise around a slender ankle.

The woman gave a cry, startled and low-throated, delivered in terror when he captured her.

As Hernando fell overboard, dragging her with him, the world suddenly became silent and slow.

His skull hit the water at high speed.

She struggled, kicking at him, but he held onto her relentlessly.

Then the big boat sped away, leaving them in its roaring wake.

Motion. His lifeless body swirled helplessly, tugged under by a powerful undertow.

There'd been no chance for a poor boy like Hernando to learn to swim in the barrio. As he sank, drifting deeper, his fingers dug into her ankle ever tighter as he fought to breathe.

He gagged and strangled.

So did she.

Salt water burned his sinus passages and filled his lungs.

She lashed out at him, kicking ever more frantically, but he held her slim limb in a merciless death grip till the last of her strength was gone.

He fought the invading water till he could fight no more.

Soon he barely felt the burning pain everywhere in his head. He barely knew that his body was churning and twisting and sinking ever deeper into the blue.

She had quit fighting now, but he held on to her limp foot and dragged her down.

If she were dead, a part of el genio *would die, too.*

For himself, he prayed for one thing—*to see Isabella's face one last time.*

Instead he saw his mother's face as she had lain in the dirt after the barrio jackals had beaten her and called them both terrible names. Instead he remembered the vow of vengeance he had taken that day.

Still, he wanted to think of Isabella, not his mother.

His daughter's face would not come.

His eyelids flickered. His eyes rolled.

Everything grew dark and silent.

Holding on to the lifeless woman, he drifted deeper until he was lost forever in the cold, blue darkness.

Cutter was pale, shivering, unconscious.

They were calling for a doctor.

"Please, dear God, please don't let him die," came the faraway, slurred sounds of a woman's husky prayer.

Her voice, weak and fragile.

Or was it?

Hot, searing pain spread through Cutter's right shoulder.

Freezing. Hungry. Cold.

Freezing. Hungry. Cold.

The sun was burning through the clouds. He could feel its warmth upon his skin even as he shuddered.

Dimly Cutter felt the peaceful lapping of the waves beneath his dangling feet as two men carried him from the boat and lowered him onto the sand. There were voices around him, in the distance, nearer, too.

He opened his eyes.

Shapes came slowly into focus. Uniforms. Both white and blue.

Then *she* was there, kneeling closer because he stirred, uncaring that her sodden white dress dragged in the sand.

When she saw that he was conscious again, her face grew radiant. Weak as he was, her beautiful smile and sparkling eyes filled him with the savage urge to live.

"I waited and waited," she breathed, shivering. "I was so afraid, so worried, you wouldn't ever wake up."

"Cheyenne, my love," he whispered soundlessly, wondering why she looked so wet and bedraggled.

She wore white. Only today her dress was plastered to her body. Her wet red hair blew in the wind as it had that day so long ago on the island when he'd fallen in love with her. Still, to him she looked like an angel.

He moved his lips, but when he tried to speak his throat burned.

"You came back," he whispered at last, though his voice was dry.

"For you," she said gently. "I would have had no life— without you. You told me once that you played by your own rules. Not some gangster's. Not mine. I guess I decided maybe I'd better show you I could do the same."

"I'm supposed to save you."

"Maybe it was my turn."

"My turn, too, Dad!" Jeremy said. "I chopped him in the neck like that Lupe guy taught me to. I was brave this time, huh?"

"Very brave."

"I thought maybe Hernando would use the Cigarette boat," she said. "We got to it first, broke the lock on the hatch and hid inside."

"He could have killed you both."

"He nearly did. He dragged Mom down. These fisher-men helped me—"

"Jeremy, hush! Cutter, darling, we were too afraid for you to care much about our own safety."

Wet strands of her long red hair blew around her face and neck. A silver light came from behind her and lit her hair like spun flame. As always there was something fragile and otherworldly and enchantingly angelic about her. He noticed that the jungle was ablaze with huge, exotic flow-ers—bold pinks, reds and blues.

She was slender and fragile. More so than usual, after her ordeal.

What kind of woman would take on a killer like Her-nando?

He had dragged her down— Cutter saw the marks on her face. She was one helluva woman. She truly loved him.

Cutter groaned as a sudden burning pain in his shoulder made him convulse.

"The ambulance is on its way, darling. There's a hospital in Quepos. Doctors. The works. You're going to be okay. As soon as you're stable they'll fly you to San José."

"So—you saved my life a second time? On a second beach."

She smiled. "And it had better be the last."

"I promise."

"Say it."

"What?"

"You know...the three words I longed to hear...for seven years."

"I love you," he whispered, touching the darkening bruise on her cheek.

"I love you, too."

"What about me?" Jeremy piped up.

"That goes without saying," Cheyenne said, pulling him down beside them, so that Cutter could touch his son's face.

"You were both great," Cutter whispered. "Great."

"You don't know the half of it, Dad! Mom—"

"Shhh—"

Men with stethoscopes were racing toward them with a litter.

Cutter's last pleading words to her before they carried him away to the ambulance were, "Don't leave me."

"As if I ever could," she said.

Thunder rumbled in the distance, and the breeze fanned them with the sweet smell of rain.

Cutter woke with a start when the balcony doors right above him were slammed open, not by the wind, but by his son.

"How come they never found Hernando's body? Do you think maybe some sharks ate him or something?" Jeremy shouted down from the balcony to the garden.

"Hold that thought," Cutter muttered with a drowsy smile, glancing up at Jeremy and the blackening sky from his chaise lounge and then lazily closing his eyes in an attempt to continue his nap.

"I've been reading about sharks," Jeremy persisted. He leaned over the balcony railing and began to sling the red yo-yo he'd bought in the flea market last week up and down. "There are lots of 'em down here. Tourists are always getting eaten or sucked away in undertows."

"Jeremy! Hush!" Cheyenne murmured, looking up from her dog-eared paperback thriller. "Hernando is dead. We are safe. Your father needs to rest. The last thing he needs is to think about stuff like that."

"I don't mind thinking about Hernando being eaten—"

"Shhh!" To Jeremy she said, "I told you to read quietly, till three when your father gets up."

"I forgot."

"Like always," she chided gently.

"Okay. Sorry. Can I go over and play with Juan then? He's got a different kind of yo-yo."

Juan lived next door.

"No," she said. "It's going to rain, and you'll be stuck over—"

"Why don't we let him," Cutter assented with a sly grin.

"Please, Mom?"

"Just this once," Cutter insisted. "He'll be okay."

Then father and son both nagged her silently with their eyes.

"All right then, but only since your father..."

Gingerly Cutter eased himself higher in his chaise lounge. A week had passed since Hernando had shot him. Cutter was out of the hospital and convalescing under Cheyenne's attentive care. She had rented a villa in the cool mountains outside San José and cooked every meal herself. The doctors said she must be a magician with soups and herbs because they had never seen anyone with Cutter's injuries improve so rapidly. When other patients had smelled her spicy casseroles and soups and begged her to bring them something to eat, and she had done so, they had quickly gotten well, too.

Today, even beneath the dark skies, the gardens and patios of the house were ablaze with oversize orchids and draperies of lush bougainvillea. Bromeliads hung from the brick walls, and a large cage by a huge philodendron vine was filled with dozens of chattering tropical squirrels.

"So many flowers," Cutter murmured lazily to his wife, when he heard Jeremy dash out the garden and slam the gates.

"Flowers are a good sign for us," Cheyenne said absently, turning a page. "Especially when so many bloom by day."

"If you say so, my darling. They certainly seem to bloom whenever you are around."

Lightning flashed in the mountains.

She didn't look up from her book. "I've told you before, I'm a talented gardener."

"You're a lady of many talents." Cutter's smile grew tender as he leaned over and teasingly snatched her book from her fingers and tossed it aside.

"I was on the last page."

"It'll wait." He sighed, growing serious. "I can't. Besides it's going to rain."

"Cutter."

"Come here. Your patient needs a little of your tender bedside care."

She smiled. "What exactly do you have in mind?"

"I think you know. You probably put something in my food just to get me hot for you."

"I did not! And you're much too badly injured to even think about sex."

"I'll be the judge of that," he said in a hard, masculine voice that was filled with sudden strength and determination.

She laughed as he pulled her down into his arms.

He suppressed a groan of pain.

"See, you're still too—"

"Pura vida," he said, ignoring the burning ache in his shoulder.

"You hate that expression."

"But I love you." His smolderingly intense eyes conveyed the same message. So did his broad grin. "I love you."

"So, what are we going to do about it, tough guy?" Her voice was barely above a whisper.

"Plenty."

In the next instant his arms were around her and his mouth hungrily possessed her lips. When she gasped with heady pleasure, she set him aflame. Soon he was holding her tight as if he intended to get inside her then and there.

A long while later he lifted his head from hers and stared at her. Gently, wondrously, he touched her face, her throat. Then he smoothed her hair. "We're going to be together, my darling. Always. We're going to live happily ever after. Just like they do in your books."

"I thought you didn't believe in happy endings," she said, beaming at him in delight as the first raindrop struck her cheek.

He continued staring at her and smiling. "I do now— since I have you."

Very gently he placed his hands on either side of her face before he kissed her again.

They were together; they were in love. After seven lonely years, they knew that nothing could ever part them again.

And because their eyes were closed and their mouths fused in a wild exultation that joined their souls, neither of them saw every flower in their garden burst into bloom.

A fierce wet wind stirred through the garden, causing them to break apart.

"Cutter! It's going to rain!"

He didn't care. He took her hand and pulled her up. As they hurried toward their house, huge, fat drops began pelting them. Thunder cracked, and then the rain began to rush down in torrents freshly watering the flowers and earth as he pulled her inside.

No way would Jeremy try to come home till the storm was over.

Gently, without speaking, husband and wife came together.

Cutter kissed her—a long, deep kiss that felt as eternal as his love for her.

* * * * *

CHILDREN OF DESTINY

return in February 1998
in the exciting Silhouette Books release

SECRET CHILD

by

ANN MAJOR

JUST TURN THE PAGE FOR AN
EXCITING PREVIEW
OF THIS SOON TO BE RELEASED NOVEL!

Chapter 1

The siren was shrill, cutting the eerie silence like a knife.

Jack West awoke with a start, his gaze as alert as a cat's as he glanced fiercely around his cheap, San Antonio, motel room. He half-expected to find himself back in cell block C, a knife-tip shoved to his throat, a murderer's legs straddling his lean waist.

He was alone.

Safe.

Even so, his heart pounded a few seconds longer, his senses having been honed by the constant danger and violence he'd lived with for the past five years.

He felt the loneliness that he had known for so much of his life close over him. It was deep and dark, but he surrendered to it, welcomed it. For he had given up on life.

The name Jack West once had meant something in south Texas. He'd been rich and famous.

No more.

Jack West. Crisp, prison-cropped black hair. Indian dark eyes with long bristly lashes, brooding eyes that could flame with hate as hot as tar-tipped torches or turn as cold as black ice and stare straight through his enemy.

Before prison he'd been tough.

He was tougher now.

His carved face and tall, muscular body were harder and leaner than ever. Scars crisscrossed his broad back from the night he'd unwisely gotten too friendly and too drunk on smuggled gin with an inmate named Brickhouse.

Jack's once healthily dark skin was sallow, but the scars on his body were nothing compared to the ones on his soul. He couldn't forget that even before his conviction, Theodora had thrown him off the ranch, seized his daughter and cut him off from his life forever. Once, he had hoped, he had almost believed, his life might count for something after all.

No more.

Jack West wasn't much different than a dead man.

He was even worse off now than when he'd been a boy—a young beggar and thief in Matamoros, Mexico. His mama had been a cheap Mexican whore; his father an Anglo ranch foreman who'd paid for five drunken minutes with her. He'd known his father's name was Shanghai Dawes only because his mother had stolen Shanghai's wallet when he'd passed out.

Jack had spent his first ten years in a shack in a dusty Mexican barrio where he'd had to steal or starve, where he'd lived on the fringes, on the bottom even there. He'd spent the rest of his life living like a cowboy prince in Theodora's big three-storied white stucco house on *El Atascadero,* one of the grandest of the great ranches in south Texas.

Jack owed his Anglo looks and great height and his talent with animals to the father he'd never known; but on the inside he was more Mexican than Anglo. He knew that because when they'd locked him up, his soul had left him. He'd watched it go.

His mother would have said he had the *susto.*

Whatever. His soul hadn't come back yet—even though they'd let him out. He didn't want it back, either.

Outside in the sweltering darkness, the ambulance raced north on San Antonio's Loop 410 North, its scream dying as if suffocated by the Texas heat.

Jack blinked, forcing himself to relax. He saw the rosy rectangle of light behind thin drapes and heard the muted roar of traffic.

There were drapes on the windows.

Real drapes.

Instead of bars.

The soft mattress and clean sheets weren't a cruel dream.

He was free.

Whatever that meant now.

Bastard from a barrio. Ex-con. Starting over at the bottom again.

He wished he could go back to sleep, but he hadn't slept through a night in years. He lay back and closed his eyes, dreading the dawn.

Yesterday, he'd been in solitary, his ankles shackled, his hands cuffed to his waist. Then this morning a guard had yelled at him to grab his bedroll. That he was moving.

Jack had been stunned when they'd driven him to San Antonio and set him free.

Nobody, not even his lawyer, had bothered to inform him about the serial killer who'd made headlines all over Texas when he'd confessed to one of the murders Jack had been locked up for.

Maybe he was free.

But he was embittered and unfit company for most decent folk. Maybe that wouldn't have mattered if he'd had a family who'd stood by him.

But Theodora had made her feelings crystal clear right from the first. Never once had she written or come to see him to say that she had changed her mind. After his conviction, he'd lost custody of his daughter, Carla, who probably hated him for killing her mother. All his letters to Carla and to Theodora had damn sure come back.

Return to sender. The guards had chanted that line aloud when they'd thrown his letters through the bars of his cell.

Theodora's betrayal had hurt more than his prison sentence. More than living like an animal in a cage.

No more. To hell with Theodora. To hell with the whole damn world. He'd started alone; he might as well end alone. Never again would he let anybody get close to him. He'd take some low job and drink till he found oblivion.

If Jack hated thinking about Carla and Theodora, he hated thinking about Chantal, his wife, even more.

For she had betrayed him in every way that a wife could betray a husband. He had taken her abuse and then her absences and infidelities for years. Until one day, she had pushed him too far.

When had the deeply rooted hate between them gotten its start? Had the seeds of it been there even on the first day when Theodora had brought him home to *El Atascadero.*

And how could a woman just vanish like that? Without a trace? For five damn years? Without a thought that her husband was rotting in prison for her murder? Without a thought for her daughter, whom she loved in her own bizarre and highly destructive way?

Not that Chantal had ever given much of a damn about him once she'd tricked him to the altar, given birth to Carla seven months later and saddled him with a baby and a ranch to run....

Jack lay in the dark a while longer, wishing he could turn off his mind and go back to sleep.

Half an hour later his mind was still festering with uneasy memories about Chantal and the sorry state of his life when the phone rang.

He let it ring.

Six. Eight times.

Who the hell could be calling that he'd want to talk to?

Nobody. Curiosity would be the sinking of him yet. He grabbed the phone, expecting a stranger.

The familiar, raspy, bourbon-slurred tone made his chest knot with a poignant rush of rage, regret and bitter anguish.

Theodora.

When his eyes filled with burning liquid, he brushed his fingers across his lashes.

"I've been trying and trying to call you, boy," she snapped, as full of venom and vigor as always, never for a second thinking he might not know her, nor caring that he might not want to hear from her. "I've been up half the night dialing this damned phone, trying to get you. As if I don't have a ranch to run come dawn. Like always, you don't mind a bit putting me to trouble."

"What the hell do you want, Theodora?"

"I've been thinking about things. About what you've been through. About the ranch. I want you to come home, boy."

"Home?" He hated how the word made his voice shake. "You never once wrote or came—" Why the hell had he brought that up? He didn't give a damn about her or about anybody now.

"I had my reasons."

"I didn't kill her."

Theodora made no apology for not believing him before. Theodora had never said she was sorry to a single soul in her whole damned life. So he wasn't surprised when nothing more came from her but a deep and brooding silence.

Her silence wrapped around Jack.

He lay in the dark, his heavy, unwanted emotions suffocating him.

He wanted to feel nothing.

He should hang up.

"You think you can just dial me up, and I'll come running back to you like I did when I was a half-starved kid and you were the grand queen of *El Atascadero?* Maybe I was once your top charity case," he muttered bitterly. "Well, not anymore, old woman. You don't have anything I want."

"So, what will you do? *El Atascadero* is the only home

you've ever known. You spent every dime you had on law-
yers. I'm the closest thing you've got to family.''

"I thought so once. I took a lot off Chantal—because of
you. So now, what the hell do you want, anyway?''

"I want you to find my daughter and bring her home.''
Jack's heart sank.

So—Theodora wanted Chantal.

"Hasn't she caused you enough grief, old woman?''

"She's my daughter. Then there's…Carla—''

"I don't want to hear about Carla—''

Silence.

"You called the wrong man, Theodora. I don't want to
find Chantal. I want to forget her. To be free of her. I lost
five years and everything I ever cared about. My daughter's
better off without an ex-con for a father.''

He lowered the phone, intending to hang up.

But Theodora wasn't about to let him off that easy.

She knew all of his buttons.

Which ones to punch. Which ones not to.

Maybe she'd get him to come back to *El Atascadero*.
Maybe he'd even find his evil wife for her.

The question wasn't whether he'd return…it was
whether he'd survive….

Take 4 bestselling love stories FREE

Plus get a FREE surprise gift!

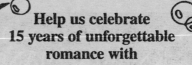

Help us celebrate
15 years of unforgettable
romance with

▼ SILHOUETTE®
Desire®

You could win a genuine lead crystal vase, or
one of 4 sets of 4 crystal champagne flutes!
Every prize is made of hand-blown, hand-cut
crystal, with each process handled by master
craftsmen. We're making these fantastic gifts
available to be won by you, just for helping us
celebrate 15 years of the best romance reading
around!

DESIRE CRYSTAL SWEEPSTAKES
OFFICIAL ENTRY FORM

To enter, complete an Official Entry Form or 3" x 5"
card by hand printing the words "Desire Crystal
Sweepstakes," your name and address thereon and
mailing it to: in the U.S., Desire Crystal Sweepstakes,
P.O. Box 9076, Buffalo, NY 14269-9076; in Canada,
Desire Crystal Sweepstakes, P.O. Box 637, Fort Erie,
Ontario L2A 5X3. Limit: one entry per envelope, one
prize to an individual, family or organization. Entries
must be sent via first-class mail and be received no later
than 12/31/97. No responsibility is assumed for lost,
late, misdirected or nondelivered mail.

DESIRE CRYSTAL SWEEPSTAKES
OFFICIAL ENTRY FORM

Name: _____

Address: _____

City: _____

State/Prov.: _____ Zip/Postal Code: _____

KFO

15YRENTRY

Desire Crystal Sweepstakes
Official Rules—No Purchase Necessary

To enter, complete an Official Entry Form or 3" x 5" card by hand printing the words "Desire Crystal Sweepstakes," your name and address thereon and mailing it to: in the U.S., Desire Crystal Sweepstakes, P.O. Box 9076, Buffalo, NY 14269-9076; in Canada, Desire Crystal Sweepstakes, P.O. Box 637, Fort Erie, Ontario L2A 5X3. Limit: one entry per envelope, one prize to an individual, family or organization. Entries must be sent via first-class mail and be received no later than 12/31/97. No responsibility is assumed for lost, late, misdirected or nondelivered mail.

Winners will be selected in random drawings (to be conducted no later than 1/31/98) from among all eligible entries received by D. L. Blair, Inc., an independent judging organization whose decisions are final. The prizes and their approximate values are: Grand Prize—a Mikasa Crystal Vase ($140 U.S.); 4 Second Prizes—a set of 4 Mikasa Crystal Champagne Flutes ($50 U.S. each set).

Sweepstakes offer is open only to residents of the U.S. (except Puerto Rico) and Canada who are 18 years of age or older, except employees and immediate family members of Harlequin Enterprises, Ltd., their affiliates, subsidiaries and all other agencies, entities and persons connected with the use, marketing or conduct of this sweepstakes. All applicable laws and regulations apply. Offer void wherever prohibited by law. Taxes and/or duties on prizes are the sole responsibility of the winners. Any litigation within the province of Quebec respecting the conduct and awarding of a prize in this sweepstakes may be submitted to the Régie des alcools, des courses et des jeux. All prizes will be awarded; winners will be notified by mail. No substitution for prizes is permitted. Odds of winning are dependent upon the number of eligible entries received.

Any prize or prize notification returned as undeliverable may result in the awarding of that prize to an alternative winner. By acceptance of their prize, winners consent to use of their names, photographs or likenesses for purposes of advertising, trade and promotion on behalf of Harlequin Enterprises, Ltd., without further compensation unless prohibited by law. In order to win a prize, residents of Canada will be required to correctly answer a time-limited, arithmetical skill-testing question administered by mail.

For a list of winners (available after January 31, 1998), send a separate stamped, self-addressed envelope to: Desire Crystal Sweepstakes 5309 Winners, P.O. Box 4200, Blair, NE 68009-4200, U.S.A.

Sweepstakes sponsored by Harlequin Enterprises Ltd., P.O. Box 9042, Buffalo, NY 14269-9042.

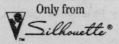